Love at a Luau

Mahlena-Rae Johnson

01. Get up and get down.
Fri afternoon, July 04, 2014

"Together forever? That's a long time."

"Are you scared that could be us?"

An insistent knock reverberated through the wooden door.

"It's open!"

KC Santana heard the knob turn. She hit the pause button on her laptop.

Lounging in gingham pajama pants and a weathered Big Apple Ivy University t-shirt, KC remained swaddled in a blanket, immobile on her new couch in her new living room, wondering how the past 34 years of her life had brought her to this place.

Swan Tutuola rolled into the sparse apartment from the hallway, holding a cloth tote bag on her lap and wearing a hibiscus-print maxi dress. She was almost 40, and this would be Swan's time to shine. The wheel on her chair kept the door ajar.

"You don't lock this, KC?" Swan asked from the doorway.

"Why bother? It's super safe here, Swan." KC accidentally bumped the open computer on the wooden coffee table.

The video restarted. Strains of Pachelbel's Canon in D

emanated from the screen.

"What are you watching?" Swan asked.

KC shut her candy-colored machine. "A fantenovela. Catching up *Mirage of the Mines*. I'm on the *Spring's Nocturne* part of the series. What's up?"

Swan took a breath. "I came to get you for the luau at Big Beach."

"Why are they doing this? What do *we* have to celebrate on the fourth of July?"

"It's a welcome party."

"Upon our arrival, I got that basket of local fruits," KC said, gesturing toward the dining table, "a refrigerator pre-stocked with my favorite foods, and a bed/bathroom suite containing the softest sheets and towels in the Northern Hemisphere. I've been welcomed."

"You haven't left this apartment since we got to the island."

KC scratched the tangled clump of dark brown curls wrapped into a sloppy bun on top of her head. "Four days isn't that long. I start my newly-assigned job on Monday, so I'll get out then."

Swan eyed her friend with skepticism. "Shira's expecting us. She's holding a table."

"Is this thing mandatory?"

"It's supposed to be therapeutic."

"I don't need therapy."

"Have you seen your assigned counselor yet?"

"Yes, and I told her I'm fine."

"You need to get dressed."

KC folded her arms. "I don't want to party. Leave me alone."

Compliant, Swan rolled herself back into the hallway.

"Where are you going?!"

Swan returned to the doorway.

"I don't have anything to wear to a luau," KC pouted. "The train's limit of one checked bag and one carry-on limited my wardrobe options. No room for packing themed party attire on the Underground Railroad."

Swan held up her bag. "I knew you would have objections." She tossed the bag at an unexpecting KC. "Shirt, pants, hat, sandals, all your size."

KC pawed through the bag. "No lei?"

"You can get leied at the beach." Swan motioned to the bathroom. "Five minutes. Go."

KC crawled off the couch cushions, lumbered to the back of the apartment, and reemerged in her new ensemble, which, as expected, fit KC perfectly. Swan knew her well.

KC donned a pair of black Ray-Bans to hold back her newly-brushed mane. "Happy?"

"You look great." Swan waved KC toward the doorway.

"Like it matters. We're going to a pity party—"

"Welcome. Luau."

"—for a bunch of shell-shocked refugees. Who's going to be checking me out?"

02. Beach blanket bingo.
Fri afternoon, July 04, 2014

"How long is this supposed to last?"

KC followed Swan and her three family members as they all disembarked from the public bus.

Swan rolled through the palm-tree-flanked main entrance of Big Beach, a community destination that spanned over a mile of shoreline along the north side of the vast lagoon in the center of the donut-shaped island.

"As long as it takes to adjust your mood," Swan replied to her friend.

"It's going to be fun," Swan's 15-year-old daughter Shalom assured.

"And if it's not," Shalom's father Miguelito chimed in, "I hear there's rum punch."

Music was playing. Families were dancing. Greeters dressed in bird-of-paradise Aloha shirts and grass skirts were placing real flower leis around the neck of the guests.

Shira Yamaguchi—52 and fabulous, in her professionally understated way—waved to the party of five from the middle of the outdoor dining area on the lawn.

Swan waved back with a big smile and headed in Shira's direction.

KC scowled at the happy couple. She turned and

skulked away from her party.

"Where are you going?" Swan called out, as a greeter placed a yellow lei over her cropped natural black coils.

"Long walk on the beach."

Swan folded her arms.

"I'll be back when the food hits the tables." KC put up two fingers and kept moving.

While Swan and her family waded through the bustling crowd to reach Shira at their table, KC shuffled along the sand toward the surf to find a lounge chair to relax in, away from the hubbub. She looked back at the servers preparing the food, peeling back the sheets of banana leaves covering the steaming holes filled with pork shanks, along with fish in a kaleidoscope of color.

KC turned her eyes to the shoreline. She cringed at the couples cuddling on the beach as the sun set on the horizon.

This paradise was KC's nightmare.

KC thought she saw two empty seats in the distance. She approached swiftly but, before she could pounce, an elderly woman and her male companion claimed her oasis.

KC grunted and continued her search.

Eventually, KC found a lone, comfy chair in a quiet area away from the crowd. She brushed the seashells off the striped cushions and lay back with her feet up.

Finally.

KC lowered her sunglasses, closed her eyes, and inhaled her surroundings.

The sea air from the lagoon.

The gentle breeze rustling the healthy fronds of the palm trees.

The aquamarine waves cresting and falling onto the white sand.

Right before KC's face could relax into complacency, her peace was disturbed by a man's bark.

"You can't sit here."

03. Sit in.
Fri afternoon, July 04, 2014

"Who are you?"

KC lifted her Ray Bans and looked the intruder over. A set of sun-bronzed, washboard abs stood in front of her face. The man's oiled torso was framed on the bottom by a low-slung circle of palm fronds around his waist. The leaves barely covered his taught pelvic muscles. A pink and white floral garland rested on his bare chest.

KC kept scanning upward to meet the man's coal black eyes.

He stuck out his hand. "Marlowe Gambon. My friends call me Lo."

"What should *I* call you?"

"Nice to meet you too," Lo said with a grin, still holding out his hand, with his bare feet firmly planted in the soft sand.

KC deigned to shake his hand. She remained stretched out on the chair. "Is this 1950s Alabama?"

"No...?"

"Then why can't I sit here?"

Lo pointed to the stage. "The program's starting. Everyone's moving to the tables. You don't want to miss out."

KC sat up. "Are you the party police?"

"Well, I do run the show."

KC gave Lo's chiseled body a once-over yet again. "What show is that?'

"I'm the entertainment. Not just me. Our dance troupe, Pikake Beats. I run it. Well, actually, Vin's in charge of the troupe. I run the whole Movement Center empire, but Vin does the artistic stuff. She's the Creative Director. And my partner. But I still dance in the troupe. We're performing tonight."

"Wouldn't want to miss that." KC pushed her sunglasses back down onto her nose and resumed her supine position, ignoring Lo.

"KC, come on." Lo held out his hand to pull her up.

"How do you know my name?"

"KC Santana. You and your Associate friends, the eight of you city planners, were all over the Homestead news talking about the network's Expansion for the past year," Lo said. "Spreading our pacific...? Pacifist...? Nonviolent lifestyle to new, sustainable communities in Brazil, Russia, India, and China."

"That's me."

"Ensuring the personal freedoms and inclusive harmony provided by Homestead for thousands—"

"Hundreds of thousands," KC corrected.

"Of new residents who have never experienced our safe environment, our emotional security, our prosperity. Until the invasion, well... you know."

"Yeah, I know. This," KC waved at the hundreds of

refugees finding their tables behind her, "is all kinda my fault."

"No one blames—"

KC stood up from the lounge chair without accepting Lo's help. She started trudging up the path back to the party and looked over her shoulder at a perplexed Lo.

She eyed down his bare torso one more time. "What kind of dancing did you say you do?"

04. Center of attention.
Fri night, July 04, 2014

"And that concludes my remarks for tonight."

"KC, over here!" Swan waved with vigor.

KC stopped staring at the man addressing the crowd and maneuvered through the dining area toward the table closest to the stage. The tablecloth had a large white RESERVED sign in the middle of the place settings.

"Again, I am your mayor of Kapualani Ranch, which I understand is where most of you have been relocated to? Is that right, Shira?"

The Mayor looked to stage left at Shira, who was waiting in the wings.

Shira, accustomed to the Mayor's lack of certainty about any issue that fell under his purview, walked across the stage toward him and spoke into the stationary microphone.

"Yes, that's correct, Mr. Mayor. Approximately 1,000 of our new residents who came from Reubenville are now living in Kapualani Ranch, and the remaining 100 who came to our island of Hale Kupua are living in 'Ohana Circle."

"Right, right," the Mayor said. "No matter which side of the island you live on, I'm your mayor; the only mayor on Hale Kupua. My door is always open, *Shira?*" The Mayor scooted off the stage and headed toward a waiter carrying a full tray of local hors d'oeuvres, on a mission to intercept the crudités into his belly.

"Okay, so..." Shira took over. "Friends. Hello. I'm Shira Yamaguchi, Executive Director of Kapualani Ranch. We are so happy to have you here."

At the head table, Shalom asked KC, "Isn't the Mayor in charge of the luau? Shouldn't he stick around?"

KC replied, "It's different than it was in Reubenville. Here the Mayor acts more like a Senator, and he represents Kapualani Ranch in the Homestead Mayors' Council. Shira functions like the governor of Kapualani Ranch and manages the town."

"But we live in 'Ohana Circle," Shalom said.

"Yes, we do."

"So who represents us?"

KC didn't have an answer for that.

Swan saw a well-dressed man scooching by their group. "Alvester?" She waved him over and quietly introduced him to everyone at the table. "Alvester Kao, this is my daughter Shalom. This is my father—"

"You can call me Poobah," he said to Alvester, shaking his hand.

"And Miguelito Desjardins. And KC Santana," Swan continued in a hushed tone, so as not to interrupt Shira's speech. "Alvester is one of my new favorite people on the island."

"He is?" KC mumbled. "We just got here."

Swan ignored KC. "Alvester works in International Relations for Hale Kupua."

"Nice to meet you all."

"Sit with us," Swan told Alvester. "Unless you have a better table."

"Better than the head table? I doubt it."

Miguelito pulled out the empty seat next to him. "Take a load off, my man. That's is what you Americans say, no?"

Alvester sat down. "Thanks. Us Americans?"

"My ex-husband grew up in France," Swan explained. "And Spain. And England."

"And you were raised in Nigeria," Miguelito countered. "But you are now very American, with this, how do you say, 'swag'?"

"It's called 'self-confidence'," Swan said.

"Don't worry. I like it."

Swan sniffed at Miguelito. "I wasn't worried."

"My dad's very European," Shalom shouted across the table to Alvester. "He thinks pizza burgers are exotic."

"Shh," Poobah said to his granddaughter. "Shira is still speaking."

"We know the events of the past weeks have left us confused, angry, displaced, and lost." Shira paced along the stage. "But you have crossed the ocean, and you're safe now, on our small island in the Pacific. You are home. Aloha."

The audience applauded.

"Shalom!"

Shalom turned her head to see two of her friends

gesturing for her to join them.

"Can I go sit with Hollis and Brooklyn?" Shalom asked Swan. "I haven't seen them since we left Reubenville."

"Can you eat something first?"

Shalom scarfed down the seafood appetizers and bolted.

Her departure left an empty chair next to KC.

From the stage, Shira continued. "In our home, we have many traditions, including the hula."

Lo's dance troupe walked across the wooden planks in a semicircle formation.

Shira asked for volunteers to join the troupe to learn and help demonstrate the traditional Hale Kupua hula. "The Hula Kupua," she laughed to herself.

The audience shrugged collectively.

"Anyway," Shira said, "who's ready to dance?"

At the table, Swan held out her hand. "KC?"

"No, thank you." KC slumped in her chair.

"Fine. Alvester?"

He shook his head. "I've never been good at the Hula Kupua. I'll guard the table."

Swan, Poobah, and Miguelito joined Shira on stage for the group luau lesson.

Alvester watched the skilled dancers attempt to guide the hoi polloi in a simple combination of arm motions, hip sways, and footsteps.

Bored with the spectacle, KC surreptitiously glanced at her last remaining tablemate. She took in Alvester's crisp buttoned-down linen shirt and pressed khaki chinos hemmed to fall at his ankles above his polished leather sandals. She avoided his dark brown eyes, complemented by nascent crinkles. But KC did appreciate that his short black hair was effortlessly styled with wisps of silver strands at his temples.

"This is really something," Alvester said.

KC rested her chin on her palm. "It would help if they tried to move in the same direction."

"That never happens."

KC nodded silently.

"What I meant was, throwing this party for over a thousand displaced people in less than a week." Alvester looked around at the tables. "And they look like they're having a good time."

KC grumbled, "They sure do."

"One more time!" Shira called out to the band, as the stage crowd muddled through the hula motions, limbs flailing.

"It must be hard," Alvester said.

"Yep."

Alvester regarded KC with concern from across the table. Then he dropped his gaze toward his place setting. "I'm not good at small talk."

KC turned to face him. "And you work in International *Relations*?"

"I can talk about deep stuff. Mixing and mingling, exchanging superficialities is not my forte."

"It used to be mine." KC pointed to the stage. "Three months, ago, I would have been shaking it up there, center spotlight. But tonight? I wouldn't have left my couch till Monday morning if Swan hadn't collected me. So, yeah. It is hard."

Alvester nodded. "I can't fully relate. I've lived here for over 20 years, and we left our previous home voluntarily. Though I've heard it gets better."

The audience applauded as the group lesson ended.

"You don't have to sit over there by yourself." KC pulled out the abandoned chair for him.

Alvester moved next to KC. "Thanks."

Swan returned to the table with Poobah and Miguelito, glowing from the exertion of energy.

Shira stayed at the microphone and introduced the next act. "New friends, Pikake Beats presents to you the Founders' Dance, which tells the story of how Kapualani Ranch was formed, danced by Marlowe Gambon and Vin Haversham."

Under the warm lights, Lo and Vin performed an intricate duet.

KC watched as the two of them weaved in and out of patterns, following syncopated rhythms. "Pretty good," she whispered to Alvester.

As the performances continued, the new residents ate served meals, their plates filled with kalua pork, ahi, white rice, macaroni salad, breadfruit, pasteles, pineapple, and poi.

Shira made her way to the table and sat down to nosh. "I've only a moment before I go back up there."

Swan brushed the dark strands from Shira's face and kissed her cheek. "You're doing a great job."

"Yeah," KC nodded. "This is *really* something." She exchanged a secret glance with Alvester, who held back a chuckle.

Shira was pleased. "I'm glad you're here," she said, between chews. "All of you. Despite the circumstances."

When the dessert combinations were served, everyone at the table received their respective bowls of shaved ice and strawberry mochi balls, but Alvester did not get a slice of coconut cake.

"And it's my favorite," he said.

The waiter shrugged. "We ran out?"

"How did you run out?" KC asked. "We're the first table."

Alvester shook his head. "It's not a problem."

The waiter departed.

KC placed her dessert plate in front of Alvester. "I like my coconut and my cake separate."

Alvester hesitated.

"I insist."

He acquiesced. "I'll make it up to you."

KC ate the mochi out of her bowl. "If you say so."

05. Welcome to the island.
Mon morning, July 07, 2014

"'OFFICE OF BUSINESS DEVELOPMENT.'"

KC read the brand new sign on the front door out loud. Wearing the lone suit that had fit in her suitcase, she observed the more casually-dressed people around her getting ready for their workdays in the town square.

She lifted up the woven mat on the wraparound porch to find the key, but the door was unlocked.

The natural light flooded through the windows of the room, which was big enough for an army of coworkers.

KC was the only one there.

She picked up the office phone next to the untethered laptop on the single desk, called Shira, and asked what she was supposed to do.

"Develop business in 'Ohana Circle," Shira answered on the other end of the line. "Same thing you did as an Associate."

"I can do that. Where's the rest of my team?" KC sat down on the single, luxurious office chair.

"You're it."

"Wait, what?"

"I know you had a whole complex operation in

Reubenville, but we run leaner on Hale Kupua."

KC looked through the barren drawers of the large desk. "Okay, well, who was in this job before me, so I can get their perspective?"

"KC, this has been an ironically fortuitous confluence of events. 'Ohana Circle has grown faster than the government in Kapualani Ranch could keep up with. The town has needed its own separate Director of Business Development, and Education and Health Care and Housing and Communications, etc., for years. Then you arrived. One slot filled. Dozens to go."

"I see."

"We're still swamped over here at City Hall. Relocating over 1,000 men, women, and children across an ocean isn't exactly a breeze. Sit tight. We'll get you a meeting with the Business Development office here in Kapualani Ranch later this week. A shipment of boxes containing all the files related to the 'Ohana Circle economy should arrive later today. Till then... er..."

"I get the picture. Don't worry, I can keep myself busy." She looked out the window onto the sleepy town square. "I've got some ideas already."

"Don't get too ambitious. I know I can be intense, but the island moves more slowly than people like us. You're not working in the capital anymore."

"Thanks for reminding me."

"I'm sorry."

"I'm fine. I'll talk to you later."

"Thanks, KC."

After KC hung up the phone, she heard a knock at the door.

KC received a delivery. She opened the padded box and pulled out a fuzzy brown coconut and a slice of white cake.

She dialed the number on the attached card.

"Hello?"

"May I speak to Alvester?"

"Is this KC?"

"I got your package. Your gift. Thank you."

"You're welcome," Alvester said. "How's your first day going?"

"It started a few minutes ago. I think your coconut will be the highlight of the day, considering I currently have no files, no coworkers, and no direction."

"That's not surprising. You're working in 'Ohana Circle, the redheaded stepchild of the two sibling family that is Hale Kupua."

"Great."

"But the fact that you actually have an office could mean things are looking up for the town. I think your presence brings the number of Homestead government officials stationed in 'Ohana Circle up to two."

KC turned on her computer. "Are you the other one?"

"I'm at Headquarters in—"

"Kapualani Ranch, of course you are."

"Disappointed?"

KC paused before she answered. "Maybe."

"We could remedy that."

"You have an idea?"

"I would suggest lunch."

KC straightened up. "I do like to eat."

"Unfortunately, I'm all booked up today and tomorrow."

"Oh." KC slouched back down.

"Would dinner be too presumptuous?"

"Over there?"

"Or there," Alvester offered. "Or, oh, I have an idea! It's a surprise."

"Are we still going to eat?"

"Yes, it's a fun dinner."

"How will I know where to meet you?"

"I'll give you the address. But," Alvester thought, "then you'll know what we're doing."

"And then I can dress appropriately."

"But it wouldn't be a surprise."

"That's a conundrum."

"Oh well. We're going to Paint and Eat."

"Paint and eat what?"

06. Paint first, eat later.
Mon night, July 07, 2014

"So, we paint pictures of apples and bananas, and then we eat courses involving apples and bananas?"

KC and Alvester strolled through the doors of the PAINT AND EAT studio, which was packed with amateur artists. Tastefully arranged fruit bowls were placed on white stools in the center of the room, surrounded by a circle of easels, canvasses, brushes, and other creative supplies.

"That's the plan," Alvester said. "I read the choice of dessert tonight is apple tart or banana crème pie."

Once they located their seats, KC thanked Alvester again for the gift. She noticed that he was nervous.

"I wasn't sure you'd say yes," Alvester said. "I am a bit older than you are."

"13 years isn't that much. I asked Swan. And you're really nice."

"So are you."

KC opened her watercolors. "How did you pick this place?"

"It's where I take all my first dates."

"Your women of choice enjoy expressing themselves artistically before eating?"

Alvester swabbed colors on his canvas. "Really, I've

only been here once, as a graduation present to my daughter. The younger one. She liked it."

"Seems to be popular with daughters and families." KC pointed her dry brush across the room, toward two girls sitting next to a woman whose features resembled theirs. A confident man glided over to join the trio. "Hey, I know him."

Alvester peered over his easel. "You mean Lo?"

KC frowned. "That's his name. To his friends."

"He has a lot of friends. Not in a made-man type of way. He has a photographic memory for people. And he's a nice guy."

"Okay..."

KC looked over at the quartet again. She recognized the woman as Vin, from the Founders' Dance duet.

"He's raising two kids on his own. We single dads have to stick together."

"Oh?" KC looked at the situation across the room one more time. Then she returned her focus to her date. "You're a dad?"

"I am a dad," Alvester confirmed.

"Cool!" KC dipped her brush in the green paint.

"Do you have any children?"

"Oh my gosh, I dropped my kids off at the pool, and I forgot to pick them up!"

"Oh no." Alvester started gathering his things. "Which pool?"

KC pressed him into his seat. "I was kidding. I don't

have any children. Not yet."

Alvester caught his breath. "Whew!"

"It was a joke. I must be feeling better. Are you okay?"

Alvester tried to calm himself. "I was having flashbacks to my younger days. Thank goodness that era is over. Forgetting a kid somewhere is the worst."

"Are yours all at home and accounted for?"

"No, they don't live here. They're grown, for the most part. The youngest one lives with his mother."

"And how'd you decide to live here? You said you've been on the island for 20 years? Did you move from one of the other Homestead communities?"

Alvester shook his head. "I got recruited after grad school. I couldn't remember applying for anything at their parent company, Synergy, but Homestead found me."

"Same here," KC nodded. "I think I went to a Hispanic MBA conference during my first semester of business school and wrote my name down on a list at a Synergy table for more information. And then, almost year after I graduated, Kimber, my boss... my former boss..." KC drifted off for a moment.

Alvester brought her back. "I've met Kimber."

KC returned. "She rolled up on me as I was leaving my office in Santa Monica, handed me a bamboo folder, and asked me if I wanted to come work for Homestead. I was like, 'I already have a job.' And she said, 'You'll like this one better.' I opened the folder to read the offer inside, which would double my salary, plus unbelievable benefits. Then I looked up, and she was gone."

"My first Homestead boss did the same thing to me."

"And here we are."

Alvester gave KC an appreciative grin. "Lucky for us." He noticed someone a few seats over waving at him. "Qiana, hey! Do you know KC?"

KC continued painting happily for the rest of the hour, while Alvester introduced her to the other people in the room whom she hadn't met yet.

"Aren't you the social butterfly," KC stated, after Alvester had run out of former strangers to bring over.

"I'm not that popular," he said. "It's a small town. And they all seemed to know you already."

"Which is why I'm in this situation," KC mumbled.

"Hmm?"

KC pointed at the kitty-cat clock on the wall. "It's almost time for our apple and banana dinner."

"I'd better finish up." Alvester held up his colorful canvas. "What do you think?"

KC looked at her date's creation, which resembled the contents of a messy baby food jar more than the original fruits they were derived from. "Let's eat."

07. In vino veritas.
Wed night, July 09, 2014

"Before we have too much wine."

Inside Sip Sip Hooray, KC placed her hands on the back of Alvester's bespoke suit, which clung to his fit body. She guided Alvester away from the other patrons at their wine-tasting event so that they could put food in their stomachs before they imbibed too much alcohol.

"Here's good." Alvester stopped at one of the empty tables holding a tower laden with plates of hors d'oeuvres.

KC adjusted her cocktail dress as she rested on the stool. Her curls were swirled into a loose bun on top of her head. She stuffed her mouth with a slice of smoked salmon on toast, followed by a smattering of stone fruits and cured meats.

Alvester picked at the options left on the silver platter. "I'd love to hear about your family. If that's not too personal."

"It's appropriate second-date talk." KC swallowed her mouthful. "Older brother, older sister, younger brother, younger sister, middle child me. Two parents, still together. We grew up in Hennessey Park, near Los Angeles. They all still live in Southern California."

"All of them? And you're here?"

"I'm here," KC said. "Let's talk about you. Where's your family?"

"My parents and siblings followed me from Philadelphia to other Homestead communities."

"Common practice."

"After I explained to them that I wasn't living in a cult."

"My parents still don't believe me!" KC laughed. "Especially now. Go on about yours. Where are they?"

"In the Madagascar community. Fontaine de la Terre. There's a large active retiree population."

KC spread soft cheese onto a round cracker. "Similar to Scooter's Landing."

"Yes!" Alvester flagged down a waiter to secure a glass of water.

"We visited both communities. At my old job; for research. What about the rest of your family? You mentioned they don't live here."

"Since my amicable divorce a few years ago, everyone is spread out. My son Mir works in Panama. He's thinking about grad school. My daughters Drew and Casey are at university. And Bastien is the baby, even at 17. He has one more year of high school. He lives with his mother. She works in External Relations."

"In Naboombu?"

Alvester choked on his beverage. "I forgot. You were an Associate. Security clearance." He checked over his shoulder. "Most people on Hale Kupua don't know—"

"Sorry. In Reubenville, everyone knew everything; even the children. About," KC whispered, "Naboombu. Willoughby. The rest of the underground communities."

"Casey's in Willoughby, at the Institute. Reubenville's a company town. *Was*." Alvester placed his hand on top of

KC's. "Wherever the next capital is built, it will probably be the same, all the citizens knowing everything about Homestead." He lowered his voice. "Naboombu would be a great place for it, but I always think—living under the ocean? —not my cup of tea."

"You get used to it, I've heard." KC wiped her mouth with a burgundy cloth napkin and placed it on the table. "So, you don't think you'll have a *Parent Trap* moment in your future? Getting back together for your kids?"

Alvester scrunched his forehead. "With my ex-wife? No. We've both moved on." He gazed at KC. "And I like where I'm headed."

KC gave him a thumbs up. "I'd cheers with you, but I need to get a glass first. And I think I'm liking where I'm headed too."

Alvester signaled for another water. "Where is that?"

"You, me, dinner this Friday?" KC's glass of water arrived.

"Cheers."

08. Let's talk about you and me.
Fri night, July 11, 2014

"I'm having fun."

KC set her bowl and spoon in the sink. She turned on the faucet to rinse her dishes.

"Don't worry about that. You can leave them there," Alvester called from the living room.

"Are you sure?" KC responded over the sound of the running water. "Everything's so neat and tidy. I don't want to mess up your space."

"I need some mess in my life."

KC padded across the hardwood floors of Alvester's luxurious two-bedroom apartment, nestled on a hillside in downtown Kapualani Ranch. Through the sliding glass doors, she could see the moonlight reflecting off the still waters of the harbor.

Alvester made room for KC on the leather couch.

"This is nice." Alvester cradled her shoulders. "How has your first, what is it, two weeks on the island been so far?"

"Better. Especially now."

He placed a tender kiss on her forehead.

KC leaned into his arm, her flat-ironed hair grazing the one open button on Alvester's wrinkle-free, monogrammed polo shirt. But she couldn't allow herself to relax. "So... It's our third date."

"What happens on the third date?"

KC looked at Alvester to see if he was kidding.

He was not.

"People usually have expectations," KC said.

"I have none."

KC crossed her bare feet on the couch. She wiped her sweaty palms onto her jeans. "I have a 90-day rule. It's new. I just enacted it, due to... reasons."

"You're being careful."

KC explained her conditions. She used hand motions and defined some phrases that were new to Alvester. "Essentially, it's everything but. Not everything 'butt'."

"I get the idea. Though you could draw me a picture," Alvester smirked.

"Coincidentally, once you get tested for STIs, there's a three-month window, then you get tested again. Most people don't know about the window."

Alvester reached for his phone. "I'll make a note."

"I'm done talking. You go."

Alvester completed his calendar entry. "Here's my short history." Alvester counted out his list of past sexual partners using one hand and had a finger left over.

KC ran down her list and needed all of her manual digits, plus a few toes.

"Good for you!" Alvester gave her a high five. "Do you

have a toe available for me?"

"You're taking all of this well."

"All of what?"

"You think you can wait three months?"

"You did say we could do other things. Either way, you're worth the wait. So let's get tested. And then get tested again."

KC eyed him skeptically. "Okay?"

Alvester reopened his calendar. "Does tomorrow morning work for you?"

09. Everything but.
Sat morning, July 12, 2014

"Thanks again for the shirt."

At the Health Center, KC waited next to Alvester in the quiet lobby, trying to get comfortable in the plastic seats.

"Looks better on you than it does on me." Alvester twiddled his thumbs. "I know I probably don't have anything to worry about but hanging out at a doctor's office has never put me at ease."

"I used to go through this at Planned Parenthood all the time."

Alvester raised his eyebrows.

"Well, not all the time. I didn't live there."

"Staying safe, I get it." Alvester paged through the mosaic of brochures spread across the side table.

"I would make up stories in my head about the other patients walking in and out of the office."

"We could play it now." Alvester looked at the receptionist behind the plastic window. "That's Wesley Barris. I was on the PTA with his father for a few years."

Then he looked at the girl filling out forms by herself in the other corner of the waiting area. "That's Famke Chaim. She's one of the best cricket players in the island's junior league. Good game last week, Famke."

She waved at him. "Thanks, Mr. Kao."

Alvester scanned the room. The only subject left was a potted plant.

"What's the next part of the game?" he asked KC.

"Doesn't work as well when you're the first ones to arrive on Saturday morning. Charades?"

"It would take my mind off of things. Although I don't think we have anything to worry about, especially considering—"

The door to the backroom swung open with a creak.

The nurse practitioner walked out holding a clipboard. "Santana? Kao?"

...

KC led Alvester out of the Health Center and into the bright sunshine. A solar-powered bus rolled past them on the quiet street.

"What do we do now?"

Alvester slid a pamphlet from the back pocket of his chinos and held it up for KC. *Everything But*?"

"Right now?"

Alvester put away the pamphlet and placed his hand on the small of her back. "How about second breakfast?"

"You're speaking my language, sir." KC pulled the pamphlet back out of the pocket. "Then we get to the butt stuff."

10. Before you leap.
Sun morning, July 20, 2014

"Engaged and married in less than a month?"

"When you know, you know."

"What are you watching?"

Swan rolled through the doorway of KC's barely lived-in apartment.

KC stopped the video before Swan could see. She clicked the computer screen over to a swords-and-sandals battle scene. *"Mirage of the Mines: Summer's Evening."*

"Another fantenovela."

"Human stories in a fantasy world."

"I remember how Noa got you into those." Swan checked the large tote bag on her lap to make sure she had her wallet.

"That's right, she did. They take my mind off things."

"I wonder how she and Morrow are doing." She put her hand over her heart. "And their twin babies."

KC moved to the kitchen to rifle through the cabinets. "Well, we have no way of knowing for five years. Excuse me. Four years, eleven months, and ten days."

"I was only thinking out loud."

KC found what she was looking for. "I'm trying not to think."

She grabbed her reusable grocery bags and dashed to the door before Swan could ask any more questions.

...

KC and Swan walked through the aisles of the 'Ono Indoor/Outdoor Market bordering the main street of 'Ohana Circle.

"Nice shop." KC looked around at the variety of grocery products on display. "Smaller than I'm used to."

Swan placed a bag of oranges into the basket of her motorized cart.

KC compared the two types of bags of rice available: brown or white. "Definitely less selection here, but not bad. I'm glad your coworker suggested we check it out."

Swan selected a combo pack of spices off the shelf.

KC examined a small bag of Homestead brand sugar. "We're not in Reubenville anymore."

Swan accelerated her cart to the next aisle, leaving KC in her wake.

Her plastic basket swinging on her wrist, KC jogged to catch up to her friend. "Okay, so, yes, I said I didn't want to think. But I will admit, it is weird not seeing you all day every day. Or everyone else."

Swan stared straight ahead, steering her cart slowly past the boxes of whole-grain cereal. "This isn't easy for me either. It's not the same, even with my family, which you know includes you, right, KC?"

"I know."

"It's a transition." Swan checked the last item off her list. "How are you holding up?"

"Surprisingly well. Alvester is so nice." KC toted her overflowing basket to the checkout.

"That's fast."

"I know, but..."

"It's been three weeks."

"Four. Three since we got here. Four since the break up. Yesterday, we went on a morning bike ride. And we've been brunching, which I love. We're taking things slowly."

"If you say so."

"What are you worried about?"

"Jumping into a new relationship? So soon after—"

"What about you and Shira?" KC challenged.

"Shira and I have been seeing each other long distance for over a year. And now we're in the same place. Which is an adjustment."

"But you've only lived in the same community for the past month, which is technically the same length of time."

KC and Swan moved forward in the line.

"I'm not trying to argue with you, KC. I'm just concerned."

"What if I saw my assigned counselor again, and she said it was okay? Would you feel better about this?"

Swan loaded her items onto the conveyor belt. "Would *you* feel better?"

KC helped Swan empty her cart. "I got this." She pushed away Swan's hands. "I got this!"

11. I'm good.
Sat afternoon, July 26, 2014

"I'm here because my friend Swan said I should come."

KC handed her clipboard to the therapist, who was already seated in a stuffed armchair.

There were two other seating options in the office: another armchair or a couch next to a translucent bay window.

"There were a lot of pages, but I answered the questions." KC selected the couch so she could see the ticking clock. 1:01. "Only 49 minutes to go. Name, age, height, weight. It's all there."

The therapist looked over the papers.

"Medical history," KC said. "Not much to report."

The therapist flipped to that page.

"One pregnancy. Zero births."

The therapist made a note then placed the clipboard on a side table.

"You remind me of my Titi Dayo. I thought of that after we met the first time. Same nose. Cheekbones. Is that why we were matched? To make sure I felt comfortable with someone who looked like me?"

The therapist listened to KC.

43

"I'm as comfortable as someone could be in this situation. Five years of solitude. No contact with anyone on the outside, or else. People have done a nickel in worse places. I get a gilded cage, located three hours south of O'ahu by boat."

KC dug her finger into a fringed throw pillow. "Does the punishment fit the crime? Does it ever? I should have known saving the world came at a price."

The therapist clasped her hands.

"Yes, it has been a tough transition. I went from building new communities around the world with the seven best friends I've ever had to stacking musty file boxes in an office all by myself.

"Yes, I do have flashbacks. The Red Spore soldiers arrived out of nowhere, answered to no one—except to their two self-hating corporate militia leaders, Peach and Nikolai—and blackmailed us into leaving everything behind. Not just me and the other Associates, and Kimber and Dr. Tom. Everyone in Reubenville. They didn't even do anything!"

Startled by KC's outburst, the therapist blinked.

KC leaned back. "Hanging out with Alvester helps me feel more normal. Yes, I do realize entering a new relationship after trauma could challenge my mental health. But I'm good. He's good for me. It's early, but I think...No, I won't jinx it."

As the time ticked away, KC's tension faded.

The minute-hand hit the number 10.

KC hopped up. She reached over to shake the therapist's hand.

"Thanks. I feel great." KC slung her purse over her shoulder. "I don't need to come back, right? I'm okay.

Aren't I?"

Before the therapist could form a response, KC walked out the door. "Yeah, I'm fine."

12. Wrap it up.
Fri morning, Oct 03, 2014

"We can't be the only people awake right now."

KC stuck her hand into the pockets of her mustard Gold & Western University hoodie. The cool morning breeze blew across the harbor through her hair.

Wearing a light pea coat, Alvester peered through the glass door of the closed Health Center. "I made the appointment for 7:00 am." He checked his titanium watch. "We've got one more minute."

KC paced in a circle on the sidewalk. "If our appointment's at 7, shouldn't the Center be open *before* 7?"

Alvester turned around to see KC wearing a hole in the cement with her stomps.

"I know we have the whole day together," KC said.

"The whole weekend." Alvester pointed at their overnight bags.

"Not like anyone's at my office to miss me on my day off."

Alvester reached for KC.

She stopped walking.

He wrapped his arms around her torso to warm her up.

"Happy 90 days," he whispered in her ear.

"Happy birthday," KC replied.

Wesley the receptionist unlocked the Center doors from the inside. "Come on in."

...

"No change."

In the private office, the nurse practitioner handed KC her results.

KC reviewed the pages. "It's all good?"

"Except for a higher pulse rate than last time, everything's fine. Same advice as last time: talk with your partner, use protection, know your status by getting tested regu—Where are you going?"

KC sprinted to the lobby with her papers.

"All clear." Alvester held out his results.

KC grabbed the bags. "Ditto. There's the bus."

She dashed off so quickly she left a cloud of dust in their waiting room.

Alvester smiled, shook his head, and followed his girlfriend out the door.

Poof.

...

"We have early check in."

KC leaned on the front desk at the Singh Along Suites Resort & Spa. "King-size bed, corner room, overlooking the beach."

The hotel clerk clicked on the computer. "I see your reservation."

"Great." KC held out her hand. "Two keys, please."

"But it's not even 9:00 am."

"Yeah. *Early.*"

"Your room might not be ready yet." The clerk picked up the phone. "I'll check with Housekeeping."

KC bounced up and down impatiently on her heels.

Alvester crossed his arms. "Has it been that long?"

"Funny. How are you this chill?"

The hotel clerk held up the key cards. "Ready."

Alvester got to them first. He stuck the card envelope in his pants pocket and signed the receipt.

KC pressed her fingers on his leather belt. "Don't make me come after them."

Alvester handed the pen back to the clerk. "Thank you for your help." He pulled up the handles on their luggage.

KC's fingers slipped off of Alvester's waist as he walked away from the front desk. She watched him roll the bags to the elevator bank.

Alvester stopped to look back at KC. "Coming?"

...

"Why am I so nervous? It's not my first time doing this."

"It's not?"

"Not even in this hotel."

Alvester clutched the sheet to his bare chest. "I don't even know you anymore."

"It shouldn't be this hard. And nothing too big."

"You just have to decide what you want."

In her fluffy, white robe, KC reached across Alvester's warm body. She switched on the lamp, brushed the empty, foil wrappers into the waste bin, and pulled the thick binder off of his nightstand.

"Where's the menu?" KC paged through the book while lying on top of Alvester.

"Is it... over here?" Alvester's fingers danced along KC's tummy, resulting in a giggle fit.

"Too many tickles!" KC laughed, as she scrambled to her side of the messy bed. She dropped the book to retaliate on Alvester's vulnerable underarms.

Unprepared for the onslaught, Alvester yelled, "Truce!" He sat up in the tangled sheets.

KC picked out the Room Service page. "I will order from the phone by the window."

Before she could crawl off the bed, Alvester held her hand. He pulled her back slowly. "Hey."

"Hey."

Alvester leaned his face close to hers. "I'm glad we're doing this."

"We've already done this. Twice. Weren't you here a few minutes ago? Whole lotta shaking going on?"

"Not the physical." He interlaced their fingers. "Us. I didn't expect this. You're good for me."

"That's what I said! To my therapist."

"You told your therapist about me?"

KC nodded.

"This is getting serious." Alvester's lips found KC's.

KC inhaled his presence, sinking deeper into the kiss.

Alvester held her up so she wouldn't fall.

She sneaked her hand under the covers. "Ready for Round 3?"

He caught her fingers. "Only part of me is. The rest of me needs a moment to keep up with you." Alvester lay back on the white striped pillows. "I'm not 35 anymore."

"34. You're doing great." KC tucked him in. "I'll let you rest. Should I order you breakfast food or lunch food?"

"I'll have whatever you're having." Alvester rolled over. He passed out immediately.

KC moved to the desk chair next to the sliding glass door. The late morning sun shone through the sheer, white curtains.

She dialed Room Service, placed her order, and was about to join Alvester for a nap when she noticed a commotion occurring downstairs in the beach dining area.

KC pressed her nose against the glass. Outside of their hotel room, she spotted Lo—the assertive dancer from the luau—and his partner Vin. The two of them directed multiple crews who were surveying the performance area, blocking their dances, and setting up the venue for an event.

After a minute of peering, KC opened the glass door to get a better view of their activities.

At the DJ booth near the front of the stage, Lo held up his hand to Vin for a high-five. "Yes! This is what I want."

"KC?"

Alvester's voice snapped KC back to her surroundings.

She closed the door.

Alvester had pulled up the sheet, enticing KC back into the disheveled, king-size bed.

She returned to Alvester's side.

"Before lunch arrives," Alvester crawled under the covers. "Let me take care of you."

KC leaned her head back against the pile of firm pillows. "Oh!"

13. Outpatient surgery.
Fri night, Oct 03, 2014

"Now it's my turn to take care of you."

"Go right ahead."

KC fed Alvester a bite of his mahi.

"Very good."

The two of them sat across from each other in a cozy spot at the Sea to Table Bistro, an outdoor dining establishment located on the retail section of Big Beach.

Alvester took the fork and continued consuming his entrée.

KC turned her eyes to the shoreline. She smiled at the couples cuddling on the beach as the moon rose over the horizon.

The cool breeze from the lagoon blew softly through the open-air restaurant, but did not disturb one strand of KC's bone-straight ponytail.

Alvester dabbed his napkin at his mouth. "I haven't had a celebration this nice in quite a while."

"Do you see more of them in your future?"

Alvester placed his hand on top of KC's. "Many more, I hope?"

"Yes."

He reached into his pocket. "That's good to hear, because I have something for you."

"But it's *your* birthday," KC said.

Alvester produced a flat, rectangular, black velvet box.

KC gingerly opened it.

"It's a key," Alvester said. "And a keychain. Obviously."

KC held it up to the light.

"I like having you near me, so you can come over whenever you like, even if I'm not home yet." Alvester timidly searched KC's face for a reaction.

KC set the key and chain back in the box. "I love it."

Alvester's shoulders relaxed. "I'm glad."

KC heard a buzz emanating from their area. She checked her purse. "Is that me?"

"I thought I'd turned it off." Alvester read the name on his phone screen. "It's Bastien."

"Take it."

"Hello?... Yes, thank you for remembering!"

While Alvester spoke with his son, KC gazed lovingly at her key. She consumed the rest of her seafood dinner.

"I love you," Alvester said into the receiver. "I miss you. I'll see you next month, okay, Sport?... Okay, love you. Bye." Alvester switched off his phone. "He called for my birthday."

"It sounds like you have a good relationship."

Alvester beamed. "We do. He was supposed to spend the whole summer with me, but he had a last-minute tour of schools on the East Coast, and then other requirements before his senior year. We're planning to meet up at my parents' place for Thanksgiving with the other kids too. Their mother gets winter break."

"Fair."

"I call them kids, even though they think they're grown. I'd love for you to meet them."

"That would be very nice."

KC and Alvester held hands above the table as they looked into each other's eyes.

Their waiter arrived at the table, cleared their plates, and asked if they were ready for dessert.

"We're ready." KC gave the waiter a wink. "And, can I order a cannoli to go, please?"

"Certainly. I'll be right back with your order."

"Do I not get to order a dessert too?" Alvester asked KC.

"It's a surprise," KC said. "Tell me more about your kids."

"They're the best!" Alvester laughed. "Four perfectly imperfect human beings. The last of a breed, literally and figuratively."

"How so?" KC leaned in.

"Figuratively, because they all have their own individual qualities. And literally, they're the last in this generation of Kaos. On my branch, anyway."

KC leaned back. "The last?"

"Four is enough. Once I get Bastien off to university, I'm done. Got that taken care of two years ago? Three years ago?"

KC's hands slowly slid off the table and into her lap.

"It was a simple procedure, short recovery. Minor aching at first, but all the parts in working order. As you well know."

KC said nothing.

"The point is, by next year, I will have sent all four of my children into postsecondary education. For *free*. Well, not free. Fully paid for by Homestead. Better than my decades of student loans, I tell you what," Alvester huffed. Then he noticed his companion's souring demeanor. "KC?"

KC couldn't move or speak. She heard a familiar tune ringing in her ears. The heat was coming closer to her face, warming her cheeks, sparks burning in front of her stinging eyes.

A fiery, frosted coconut cake, filled with close to 50 smoky candles, descended on the table, carried by waiters continuing their first verse. "Happy birthday, dear Alvester. Happy birthday to you!"

14. You were right.
Fri night, Oct 03, 2014

"Make a wish."

KC said her line on cue, eyes trained on her wringing hands.

Befuddled by KC's mood swing, Alvester blew out the candles.

The wait staff, along with the other restaurant patrons, cheered.

"This is quite a surprise." Alvester tried to wave away the smoke emanating from four-dozen candles.

"Your dessert to go." The waiter set a doggie bag containing the Italian pastry on the table. "And when you're ready." The check was placed on Alvester's side.

KC swiped the billfold. "You don't want any more children? Never ever?" She stuffed a wad of cash inside to pay for dinner.

"No." Alvester looked at KC with tenderness. "I didn't know that you wanted—"

"Why didn't I ask you about that?" KC directed the question to herself. "I asked you about everything else. Everything."

"This doesn't mean that—"

KC pushed her padded chair back with a piercing

scrape across the restaurant's reclaimed wood floor.

Alvester got up. "KC, wait."

She inadvertently jostled the table as she rose from her seat, knocking a half-full glass onto the tablecloth and spilling ice water onto Alvester's tailored suit pants.

"I can't do this. Not again." KC picked up her clutch. "I'm sorry I'm breaking up with you on your birthday."

The room was silent.

All the other diners were stunned, either gasping at the drama or desperately averting their eyes.

Even the waiters had stopped moving.

Alvester stood still, the water soaking his leg.

"I can't." KC walked out of the restaurant with a confused determination.

She left the key and took the cannoli.

KC walked all the way from Sea and Table down the brightly-lit path running along Big Beach to her nearby building, San Marino Bravo.

KC knocked on Swan's apartment door. Her fake eyelashes had traced a tear-laden mascara trail down her cheeks.

When the door opened, KC held up the crumpled doggie bag. "I took his dessert."

Swan remained puzzled. "What happened?"

"Thank you for being my family."

15. For real this time.
Sat morning, Oct 04, 2014

KC woke up on Swan's couch under a heavy blanket, wearing her outfit and her makeup from the night before. Her eyelids kept sticking together.

Dazed and confused, KC checked her purse for her phone. Through her coagulated eyeliner, she blinked at the screen. "How am I up this early on a Saturday?"

From her slumped position, KC surveyed her surroundings. The other members of the household were still asleep.

KC picked up her phone again. She knew what she had to do.

KC typed the following message as quickly as possible:

"Sorry for texting you at the butt-crack of dawn, but..."

She hesitated.

Then she soldiered on.

"Do you have an appointment available today?"

...

Freshly scrubbed and draped in her comfiest clothing, KC sat down on her therapist's couch, ready to work.

"So, I'm not fine."

The therapist listened.

"The whole island probably knows by now, but in case you're not up on the latest *chisme*, I ended my relationship with Alvester last night. It wasn't even his fault. He's not Topher."

The therapist tilted her head.

"Topher's my ex. One of many. But he's *the* ex. The one who had the unfortunate privilege of dumping me during the evacuation."

The therapist nodded.

"He was the most beautiful man. Model quality. Print work, not necessarily runway. That nonthreatening, racially ambiguous, but not too ambiguous look. Beige. And those eyes. Unfair."

KC crossed her arms. "All this sounds superficial, but there was more to it than his outward appearance. He had a way about him. A quality. He was super smart like us, the Associates. But it wasn't the only thing about him. I'm not explaining this well."

The therapist motioned for KC to continue.

"Love at first sight wasn't accurate. Not even lust. It was like looking at the sun. You're gonna get burned.

"On our first date he told me, 'I think I could fall in love with you.'" KC threw up her hands, shook them around, and dropped them back on top of her thighs. "What even is that? How dare he. How could someone like him want me? I'm a California 6. Homestead 8. He's, like, untouchable. In a good way.

"Then, after Noa and Morrow's wedding last year, things got complicated. We kept moving forward until Reubenville was sacrificed to protect the rest of

Homestead. I know it was the right decision, not like I was the one who made it, but I can't help but wonder... If the Mayors' Council had given us more time, could we, me and Swan and Noa and Morrow and everyone, could we have found another way?"

KC ran over those thoughts inside her own head.

The therapist waited for KC to find her words again, which took a while.

"Yadda yadda yadda, here we are. More precisely, here *I* am. Clearly, he's elsewhere. Like I said, it's a long story. Alright, I didn't say that out loud. But I thought it.

"I thought Topher would be my new family if I gave up my old family. And then after that didn't happen, when I came to Hale Kupua, I felt like I was finding new family. With Alvester. I must have wrecked him. Or not. He had the hotel deliver the suitcase I left in the room to my building. It was sitting outside my door with a note in his handwriting.

"I'm not an Associate anymore. I was never Topher's fiancée. I'm not Alvester's girlfriend. Who am I?"

The therapist was about to make a suggestion, but KC supplied her own answers.

"I need to live the life I have now. Even though this isn't a huge island, there's a ton of stuff to do. I've done some of it with Alvester. I can do the rest by myself, or with Swan and Shira and the rest. Or I could make new friends. Ones that I don't sleep with and then dump on the same day."

KC began creating a list on her phone of opportunities to explore on Hale Kupua.

As she was reading them off to the therapist, the clock on the wall hit the 50-minute mark.

KC gathered her belongings. "This was good. Thank you! Pencil me in for the same time next Saturday."

She headed for the door. "Maybe I should incorporate more movement into my schedule? Be healthy?"

The therapist was about to formulate a response, but KC was already ahead of her.

"I'll think about it. You think about it too. 'Cause I'll be back."

16. Sand in places.
Sat morning, Oct 11, 2014

"Oy."

"Again, lift your leg like a poodle on a hydrant."

"With the poodles already."

"What was that?"

"Nothing." KC responded to Vin, who was walking through the other students stretched out across a wooden platform outside the Big Beach Community Center. All of them were posing on their hands and knees on rubber exercise mats, strengthening their thighs.

All of them except KC.

"Lower your leg. Let's move into plank position and prepare for our final sun salutation," Vin said, keeping her eyes on KC, who was struggling to move through the vinyasa. "Push up position."

KC bent her arms to balance her body, but her belly flopped to the mat. Granules of sand stuck to her chin.

"Strength and focus. Upward facing dog," Vin called out.

KC attempted to mimic the effortless execution of her fellow students, to no avail.

"And downward-facing dog."

"Finally," KC groaned to herself. As she arranged her hands and feet on the mat to make a triangle with her bottom in the air, she felt someone's fingers adjusting her back. "Eep!"

"I didn't mean to startle you," Vin soothed, as she corrected KC's stance. "Is this your first class?"

KC tried to make eye contact with Vin as her head hung upside down. "I've done it before, but not for a while."

Vin spread KC's toes further apart on the mat. "It takes time to get back to what you're used to."

The class moved through a combination that led them into child's pose. Once then rested into their final savasana, KC could unwind. "Relaxation," she whispered to herself, as she lay her back down on her mat, toes pointed up to the clear, blue sky. "This is the best." She inhaled and exhaled along with her neighbors.

"KC," Vin said from the front of the class, seated on her own mat.

KC opened her eyes. From her reclined position, she angled her head and saw the other students all sitting up with their legs crossed.

Apparently, KC had gotten too relaxed.

"You were snoring."

KC scurried to get into lotus position, couldn't keep her calves in place, then settled for cobbler's pose, sitting with the soles of her feet pressed together.

Vin placed her own palms together, closed her eyes, and bowed her head to her students. "Namaste."

KC returned the bow. "Namaste."

As the other students exited the area, Vin helped KC

fold her mat. "How are you feeling?"

"Sweaty. Sandy. Achy."

Vin toted the mat to the equipment shed on the Community Center porch. "You're doing great."

KC sucked down the water from her metal bottle. "You have to say that so I'll come back to your class next week."

"Please do! It gets better."

"That's what I hear." KC kept gulping her liquid. "How long have you been teaching?"

"Since university. It started as a lark, helping other dancers find calm between auditions. I didn't have time to do it regularly while I was on tour. But since I came back to Hale Kupua a few years ago to help Lo build The Movement Center in Kapualani Ranch, I decided to teach this beginner's course on my days off."

KC swallowed. "Beginner's?"

Vin patted her shoulder. "You're doing great! And you look like you're holding up well after what happened last... Never mind."

KC rolled her eyes with amusement. "I was specifically instructed not to draw attention to myself after the evacuation. Yet three months later, I make myself the center of hot goss for the island."

"It's not that bad."

"What have you heard?"

Vin shrugged. "Only that Alvester asked you to move in with him."

"Really?"

"And then you smushed a piece of cake in his face?"

"That is not accurate."

Vin nodded. "Fallacies have a way of spreading faster than facts around here."

"It's common," KC shrugged. "I've had to be corrected about things I've thought before."

"Like what?" Vin started walking to the porch so that the next exercise class could set up.

KC followed. "Like everything? To relate it to the situation, when I saw you at Paint and Eat a few months ago, I thought Lo's daughters were yours. Since he said you're partners."

"*Business* partners," Vin laughed. "It's a common mistake. At least you didn't presume he's my boss, which he is not, even though people always think that. Other people. Even though I graduated ahead of him, and I have more education and experience."

"People are terrible."

"And not all Indians are related. Although, technically, Snow Belle and Nala and I are related. All the founding families are by now. And I see them constantly. But I am not their mother."

"Duly noted."

"Me a mom? When would I have time to raise a baby? Or two girls starting puberty? I have things to do. Like my book club! Do you want to come? It's on Thursday night, if you're not busy."

"I don't read. I can read, but I choose not to." KC grumbled to herself, remembering she was supposed to be getting a life. "Okay, maybe. What's the book?"

"Let me check." Vin swiped through her phone. "I forget the title, but it's a memoir of a fantenovela star."

KC lit up. "Which one?"

Vin kept swiping. "She starred in a bunch of old shows.

"Which ones?" KC demanded.

"*Wonderkiller: Wheel of Light*?"

"I haven't seen it."

"*Aerda Dust and the Holy Claw*?"

KC leaned over to see the phone. "I think I we watched it when we visited Lake Elmo?"

"And she's directing the *Mirage of the Mines* series?"

"Cardiss Chisholm?" KC's mouth dropped open. "*The Fantasy of My Reality*?"

"Yes! That's her book." Vin showed her the cover art that featured a picture of Cardiss in the center of a swirling galaxy of stars.

KC whipped out her own phone. She opened her calendar. "Name the time and the place. I'll be there."

17. Big business.
Tue morning, Oct 14, 2014

"It's open!"

From behind her desk, KC craned her neck to see who was opening the door to her still barely occupied office.

A man walked into the room.

"Hey... there," he said. "Good morning."

It was Lo.

"Hey." KC stood up from her desk. She smoothed her dress pants. "How can I help you?"

KC watched as Lo waded through the boxes of documents stacked in large piles all over the floor.

"I think I'm in the right place." He stepped over an overflowing cardboard container. "I'm Lo. I don't know if you remember, we met at the—"

"I remember."

Lo stood in front of KC's desk. He stuck his thumbs in the waistband of his sweatpants. "Last year, I filed an application to expand the Movement Center in 'Ohana Circle, but I hadn't heard anything. So today I went back to the Business Development office downtown in Kapualani Ranch, and they directed me here."

"Did 'they' tell you where you could find your application?"

"In one of the boxes marked ''Ohana Circle'.''

KC waved her arm across the hundred-plus cartons scattered throughout the room. Each box top had the words ''Ohana Circle' scrawled across it.

Lo put his hands on his hips. "Huh."

"Since the migration in July, the 'Ohana Circle Business Development office has become the government depot for all things related to 'Ohana Circle business," KC said, checking the boxes closest to her desk, "including Education, Health Care, Parks and Recreation, Transportation, and," KC pinched open a file folder laden with dust bunnies, "Waste Management."

"This," Lo nudged another box with his flip-flopped foot, "is a lot."

"The boxes keep coming, but they do not arrive with additional personnel to unpack them. Still just me."

"I don't want to step on anyone's toes, but would you mind if I looked through these to see if my application is in here?"

"Be my guest. Though it may take less time to fill out a new one."

"Trust me, it won't. And I've got time." Lo pushed boxes out of his way to clear a space to one of the empty desks. "I'm the boss."

"What about Vin?"

"I'm the co-boss." Lo stood at the desk next to KC's. "Is there a system you've worked out for these files?"

KC pointed to a mildewed pile in the far corner of the room. "Grossest one's farthest away from me."

"Got it."

KC settled back into her important typing work on her computer. She tried to focus on her screen and not get distracted by Lo's box calisthenics. She couldn't help but notice his toned arms barely straining as he lifted three at a time, his back muscles rippling through his soft, cotton t-shirt.

"So..." KC breathed. "You're expanding The Movement Center to 'Ohana Circle?"

"That's the plan."

"Too much of a commute?"

"For me, no. I live up the street from here, in the Windhoek cluster?"

KC nodded. "I'm in the San Marino cluster."

"Yeah, so we're both really close to downtown. But many of the older citizens on the island are moving to the far east side of 'Ohana Circle. They're going past the farms that my parents run, even past the 'Ohana Circle School, because it's more laid back."

"More laid back than this?" KC pointed at the window toward the town square. A lone pedestrian strolled past a tumbleweed.

"Well, it's quieter. And these citizens still want to stay active. And there's a lot of them. So we're planning to keep most of the younger dance and choreography classes at the Kapualani Ranch Center and transfer more of the low-impact fitness classes targeted at our aging population to the 'Ohana Circle location." Lo ransacked a file pile. "If I can find the forms. Are you really running this office by yourself?"

"Don't think I can handle it?"

"I think you should ask your friend Shira for help. Have her authorize a budget for a support staff. Don't let Shira take advantage of you because you're a grateful refugee."

"I am grateful. Not everyone else who moved here got a placement right away."

"But this is a big step down from Homestead International Expansion Associate. Tell her you need a real office with real people. She'll give it to you."

"You sound confident, as usual," KC poked. "How are you certain of this?"

"I keep my ear to the ground."

KC leaned back in her desk chair. "You've got it all worked out."

"Not even. I'm not an expert at any of this. I'm a dancer who had an idea, and I wrote it down, and now I can't find it."

"Most people with an idea don't even write it down. You filed the paperwork. And, now that I'm in charge, I'm here to help you out. We can *develop* your *business* in *'Ohana Circle* together."

"That's nice of you."

"It is literally my job." KC pointed to the sign on the front door.

"Since you're helping me, how can I help you?"

"I don't have any pressing hula needs, so..."

"I have other talents."

"You do?"

"I surf."

"Eh?"

"I have a black belt in three different martial arts."

"Impressive, but…"

"I can cook."

KC leaned forward. "Go on."

"Vegan dishes, mostly."

"Oh." KC returned to her typing.

"They taste good! And they're healthy."

"I'll take your word for it."

Lo moved onto another box. He sat with it on the floor.

KC turned back around. "Are plant-based diets a big thing here?"

"I wish. My parents still serve pork or fish at every meal, which makes my kids happy. Hale Kupuans are pescatarians."

"And porkatarians."

"Except me. I only eat meat on my cheat day. Which is when I surf."

"Active lifestyle. This is the place for it."

"What do you think of the island so far?"

KC stopped her work to answer Lo's question. "Small."

Lo bristled. "It's not what you're used to in the big city."

"It's not a bad thing. By itself, Kapualani Ranch has a

larger population and a larger area than Reubenville has... Had."

Lo looked at KC with sympathy. "Yeah."

"Simple answer: good. The island is good. Despite recent tumultuous personal situations."

"You look like you're holding up well. All things considered."

"What have you heard?"

"Nothing much." Lo stuck his head in a new box. He busied himself with shuffling through papers.

KC stared at him.

Lo folded. "Only that Alvester asked you to marry him."

"And?"

"You threw a pie in his face."

"That is not accurate."

"Worse things have happened at Big Beach. I promise you, the rumors will pass."

KC pouted. "Eventually."

"Tomorrow, someone else will do something ridiculous —probably The Mayor—and everyone will forget about your pouring a glass of Chardonnay over Alvester's head."

"That's not what happened."

"Every person on the island has at least one embarrassing story that they can never live down. Worst case scenario: this is yours."

KC crossed her arms. "What's yours?"

"Too many to count. Before I went to university, I can't tell you the number of times I fell on my face in public, vomited in public, broke a bone in public, other bodily functions. And after I returned home with two kids, that was the talk of the town for years."

"You're saying this will blow over?"

"Probably already has."

"Then you've helped me out already."

"Nice!" Lo held up his hand for a high five.

KC bent down to slap his palm. "So... what other embarrassing things have happened at Big Beach? How many of them have involved The Mayor?"

Lo grinned. He tented his fingers. "Where do I begin?"

...

"Then she said, 'I've never been to Minnesota.'"

"What?!" KC burst out into guffaws.

Wiping away his own tears of hilarity, Lo sat next to her on the floor, surrounded by newly-labeled containers. "It wasn't that funny!"

"Then why are you laughing?" KC handed him a tissue as she tried to collect herself.

Lo dabbed at his wet cheeks. "Why are you?"

A buzzer sounded on KC's computer.

KC reached up from the floor to switch off the alarm. "Noon already?"

Lo stood up and dusted off his pants. "Lunchtime." He

held his hand out to pull up KC.

KC let him help her up. "I know you put all this work in, and I don't want to say 'I told you so,' but it may be easier for you to fill out a new—"

Lo placed a thick manila folder on KC's desk. "I found it in the M box an hour ago. I organized the rest of the files by name, type, and date."

KC looked around the room. The file piles had transformed into neatly-arranged stacks. It was a completely different office.

She opened the folder. "Maybe you should be on my staff."

Lo headed for the exit. He stopped and turned around before walking through the door. "You couldn't afford me."

18. Take a look.
Thu night, Oct 16, 2014

"Sandra, Ruth, Sonia, Elena, Miss Patsy, Miss Shirley, Eleanor, and Maxine. And Vin."

"That's right!" The assortment of ladies applauded KC in the common room of the Asuncion C apartment building.

"Good job, KC." Elena nodded at her.

"It took me months," Miss Patsy said, "and I still don't know some of y'all's names."

Sandra stood up to conclude the official book discussion. "Let's eat."

The group members fixed themselves plates at the potluck buffet and then walked across the room to sit back down in the circle of folding chairs.

Vin set her plate down on top of her copy of *The Fantasy of My Reality*. She answered the phone ringing in her pants. "Hello?... I'll be right there."

"Where are you going?" KC asked.

"To get a surprise." Vin walked out of the room, past Eleanor and Maxine who were lingering at the buffet table.

As Eleanor balanced her heavy-duty paper plate in one hand, she shuffled through a half-full food carton. "There aren't any sliders."

"The 'Ono Market ran out," Maxine informed her. "And the beef was double the price."

"But I eat little burgers at book club every month," Eleanor whined.

"Then next time B-Y-O-B," Miss Shirley shouted from the circle. "Bring yo' own beef."

Eleanor frowned. "All these new people. Coming here, raising up the prices." She turned to the circle. "But you're one of the good ones, KC."

"That's not okay, Eleanor," Sonia said. She patted KC's knee. "She can be a little touchy."

KC ate her clementine salad.

"I'm not the only one who feels that way," Eleanor replied.

"I remember how hard it was for my family," Miss Shirley reminisced, "the first of my kind to venture to the island, back in the day. There weren't enough of our people to fill this room. I can empathize with the new Hale Kupua citizens."

"More new citizens may be on their way," Sandra predicted, "depending on new developments."

KC shuddered. "Another invasion? From Red Spore?"

"No, Homestead is safe," Sandra said. "For now. There may be a reorganization of the Mayors' Council. Nothing definite, but I've heard rumblings."

KC tried to steady her hand, but her fork kept shaking.

Maxine faced Eleanor. "So, you don't want to share our island with our fellow Homestead citizens? The tired, poor, huddled masses who have been terrorized by outside forces for living in peace?"

"That's not what I said at all."

"Where did Vin go?" Ruth tried to change the subject. "What's this surprise?"

"Eleanor, that's what it sounds like," Sonia agreed.

Eleanor shook her head. "You're twisting my words.

"Straighten them out," Maxine said.

"If these people hadn't been dispatched here," Eleanor hissed, "this island wouldn't be in the mess we're in."

"Oh my gosh." Maxine darted back to the circle of chairs.

Tears were spilling down KC's cheeks.

"Look what you've done," Maxine said to Eleanor, who rushed back over to the group.

KC trembled with quiet sobs while the club members hugged her.

"I'm sorry." Eleanor kneeled down to worm her arms around KC within the group hug. "I didn't mean what said. I get angry when I don't have my proteins."

"We want you here, KC." Maxine squeezed her harder. "Well, I'll speak for myself."

"And for me," Sonia hugged.

"And me!" Eleanor asserted.

KC choked out a whisper. "It's my fault."

Eleanor swatted the other arms away from her victim. She gripped KC's shoulders. "It's not. None of it. This started long before you all arrived."

"We've always had shortages on some items," Sandra concurred.

"But over the past few years," Eleanor said, "they've become more frequent. The migration exacerbated the problem."

"The population is growing," Sonia said.

"Especially in 'Ohana Circle," KC sniffled.

Eleanor used her thumb to wipe away KC's tears. "I shouldn't have blamed you. That is not 'ohana."

"Surprise!" Vin burst into the room, with a guest.

Cardiss Chisholm, proud author, walked in holding out a serving dish overflowing with steak kabobs. "Straight from the outback! Premium flank from the finest Australian cattle."

Then the two of them noticed the somber mood.

Vin approached her huddle of friends. "What happened?"

...

"I want to encourage more actresses to explore their power behind the camera, so they can craft their own stories in their image. And that's why this book means so much to me," Cardiss concluded, standing in the middle of the circle.

All of the members applauded with gusto.

"I am truly inspired," Sonia said.

Maxine dangled a kabob in front of Eleanor, who remained so ashamed of her behavior that she couldn't even look at the skewered beef.

"You all are too much," Cardiss said. "And I better see you all on Saturday night. I didn't travel all the way from Lake Elmo to speak to an empty room."

"I know, I'll be there," Vin assured.

"What's on Saturday?" KC asked.

"The watch party at the Big Beach Community Center," Sonia said.

"For the premiere of *Mirage of the Mines: Autumn's Nightshade*," Vin said. "Cardiss is introducing the show."

"Then I'll be there too," KC declared. "So much fantenovela talk in such a short period of time. This is almost too much fun."

"Despite the antics of some of our members," Sandra said to KC.

"Really though," Vin asked again, "what happened?"

"I'm sorry!" Eleanor cried, chastened.

Sandra continued, "We hope you come back, KC."

KC held up her phone. "I've already ordered the next book."

19. Shop talk.
Fri night, Oct 17, 2014

"I can get it."

KC stepped away from the kitchen in Swan's apartment to open the front door.

"I'm here, I'm here," Shira wheezed from the door as she gave KC a hug. "It feels like I haven't seen you in so long."

"That is what I said to Shalom, no?" Miguelito gestured to his daughter. "And she lives next door to me."

Shalom poured herself a glass of hibiscus tea. "Mom complained that we've all been moving in different directions for weeks."

"Months," Poobah said.

"Hence, our Friday night dinner," Swan said from the kitchen.

Shira walked over to give her a kiss. "Sorry I'm late."

Poobah gave Shira a hug. "You're right on time. Here's a bowl."

"Have some stew," Miguelito offered.

Once the six of them sat down at the dining table, Swan announced that she wanted them to discuss current events instead of work. "I get enough stress at the hospital, untangling the bureaucracy. What are you all

83

doing outside of your jobs?"

KC shrugged.

"Football," Miguelito said. "In the rec league. Although, coaching football is my job. Along with the daily language class required for every new Homestead resident."

"Which one are you taking?" Shira asked.

"Tagalog," Miguelito said. "Even though I speak Spanish, French, English, German, Italian, and Japanese."

"That last one's a stretch," Swan said.

"You don't know everything about me."

"Don't I?" Swan replied to her ex-husband.

"And now," Miguelito continued, "learning how to coach football *again* is part of my job. Which I understand, because working with children in the Homestead Junior League is different than leading a professional club to a string of winning seasons in the Premier League. But who am I to—?"

Miguelito was about to finish his thought, but then he saw Swan frowning at him, and he decided against it.

Poobah broke the silence. "Shira, what's new with you?"

"My current events all involve the growing need for expansion in Hale Kapua, exposed by the influx of 1,000 new residents at once," Shira said. "And I was going to tell KC that I got her email with her request for the office."

KC piped up, "Yes?"

Swan narrowed her eyes.

Shira shook her head. "But it can wait."

"Would it take that long to tell me now?"

"Swan's house, Swan rules," Shira said.

"I don't have a job. I'll go," Shalom volunteered. "Starting 11th grade at a new school is easier than I thought it would be. Everyone's super nice, and it's not as hard as when I started 9th grade in Reubenville because I've gotten used to the Homestead educational system."

"'Educational system.'" Miguelito transferred the remaining serving dishes from the kitchen counter to the middle of the table. "This vocabulary. She *is* learning a lot."

"Poobah, what have you been doing, since you're unemployed like me?" Shalom asked.

"I'm retired," Poobah corrected. "I've been keeping busy with Listen to the Land. It's similar to the Girl Scouts, but   for   seniors."

"I was a Girl Scout," KC said. "A Brownie. There were badges."

"We don't sell cookies, but we do meet during the week in the Yellowtail cluster, on the east end of 'Ohana Circle. Peaceful. Full of nature. We learn about sustainability and survival skills. This week our instructor taught us how to trap, clean, and cook our own food."

"Like fish?" Shalom asked, spooning stew into her mouth.

"Yes, and animals native to the land as well," Poobah said.

KC speared a chunk of meat in her bowl. "What animals are native to Hale Kupua? Wasn't the island barren before the towns were founded?"

"Native is relative. But some of the oldest species here include chicken—"

"I like chicken." Swan nodded and ate her stew.

"Wild hogs—"

"I've seen them," Miguelito concurred between bites.'

"And island rabbits."

"So cute!" Shalom said, as she served herself more stew.

"And so plentiful. Easy to trap. Makes a tasty stew."

The rest of the diners dropped their spoons.

Poobah ladled more of the mixture into his dish. "More for me."

"Anyone else?" Swan looked around the quiet table. "What's new with you, KC?"

"Getting involved," KC said. "Book club last night. Yoga, therapist, and premiere party tomorrow. The only other thing I'm doing is waiting to hear back from Shira about my requests."

Swan tossed her hands in the air. "I give up. Shira?"

Shira looked over with her mouth overflowing with salad. "Hmm?"

"What do you have to share with KC?" Swan asked.

Shira swallowed her vegetables. "I received your requests. I plan to approve them next week."

"*C'est tout?*" Miguelito asked.

"*¿Es todo?*" KC echoed.

"Yeah, that's all," Shira confirmed.

KC replied, under her breath, "Told you so."

Swan put down her fork. "I heard that."

Poobah held up the half-full cauldron for the table. "More stew?"

20. Sweet fantasy.
Sat night, Oct 18, 2014

"That's the end?"

"Tune in next week."

KC wriggled in her cushioned theater seat. "What if I can't wait that long?"

Vin pointed to the white and green EXIT sign glowing over the doorway in the dark Community Center auditorium. "You could catch Cardiss before the book signing and ask her what happens next."

"Or I could tell you what happens next," Eleanor suggested, from the seat next to Vin. "These shows aren't exactly unpredictable."

"Then why do you watch them?" Maxine asked, stretching next to Eleanor.

"They're fun," Eleanor said. "I like fun."

The movie screen faded to black. The sconces along the sides of the auditorium illuminated the room."

"Are we all staying for the after party?" Sonia asked her row of friends.

KC saw the streams of people pouring into the lobby. "I should go to the bathroom first. I'll meet you all in there."

...

As she washed her hands, KC looked in the mirror that ran along the length of the sink counter in the Women's restroom. She was surprised.

She looked happy.

KC dried her hands. She opened the doors, threw the paper towel in the recycle bin, and stepped into the hallway.

"Hey, I know you."

KC turned around. She couldn't help but grin. "I didn't take you for the fantenovela type."

The Men's room door swung shut behind Lo. "My daughter's Nala; a big fan. She's getting her book signed by the director."

"Where's your book?" KC asked Lo.

"Where's yours?" Lo countered.

"At home on my nightstand, autographed with a personal message to me from Cardiss."

"Aren't we fancy? What'd did you think of the show?"

KC leaned her back against the wall. "Comforting."

Lo stood closer to her. "How so?"

"No matter how much things change, fantenovelas stay the same. The heroine always solves the murder mystery, despite the evil foes trying the thwart her path. But she vanquishes them in the end."

"What about the handsome prince?" Lo leaned his head against the wall near KC. The hallway was silent except for their voices. "How does he fit in?"

"He's an appendix. Unnecessary for the survival of the

heroine, occasionally causes trouble, but people complain when you take him out."

"A little trouble is necessary for a little fun."

"Is that your take on the situation? Of fantenovelas?" KC clarified.

"Me, myself, personally? I've never solved any murder mysteries. But I have vanquished foes."

"I've caused trouble. And here I am."

"It's a good place to be."

KC faced Lo, whose nose was a few inches away from hers. "Seems that way."

"Dad?" One of Lo's daughters stood a few yards down the hall, clutching a book.

"Nala!" Lo moved away from the wall and waved his daughter over to join them. "This is KC. She's helping me expand The Movement Center into—"

"I got my autograph." Nala didn't move from her spot.

Lo walked slowly toward her and away from KC. "Did Cardiss write something cool?"

"I guess." Nala scowled, flicking her flat-ironed hair behind her earlobe.

Lo stepped closer to inspect her reddened ear. "Is that a burn? Did you do that with your hot comb?"
"Dad, it's fine." Nala batted his hand away. "This party's boring. I'm going to get Snow Belle and go home." She walked back toward the noisy crowd.

Lo followed her. "You can't leave by yourselves, you're only 10." He turned back to KC, who was observing the discussion from the wall.

She shrugged with a smirk.

"See you later?" Lo said, ambling backward along his daughter's path.

KC gave him a nod. "Later."

21. Shower with approval.
Tue morning, Oct 21, 2014

"I'll check it again. Thanks, Shira. Bye bye."

KC hung up the phone. Sitting alone in her office, the morning sun shining through the windows, she clicked on her desk computer. An email popped open on her screen.

"Well then."

KC tapped her manicured fingernails on the desk. Then she tapped her ruby-red Mary Janes on the floor.

She picked up the desk phone again. Then she put it back down on the receiver.

She checked a map on her cell phone, slung her leather purse over her shoulder, and walked out the door.

...

KC departed the local bus and walked through the teeming sidewalks of Downtown Kapualani Ranch.

Her red slippers carried her along the road to The Movement Center. KC knocked on the door.

"Hello?" The door was unlocked. KC walked inside the empty studio. She looked at the photos and awards and trophy-filled glass cases covering the walls.

KC heard a door squeak open in the back of the building.

Lo appeared from the darkness. He padded down the hall toward KC as he toweled off his thick, wet hair.

"Hey! I was in the shower."

"Hey!" KC breathed heavily.

Drops of water rolled down Lo's bare, glistening chest. His black sweatpants hung low on his hips.

"Sorry about the other night." Lo tossed his towel onto a sparring dummy. "Nala was acting weird. Although that's not unusual for her."

KC watched a bead of sweat slide down Lo's neck, traveling past his collarbone through the wispy hairs between his pectoral muscles.

"She's never been as friendly as her sister," Lo explained. "Snow Belle likes everyone, which presents its own problems."

KC studied the perspiration journeying down Lo's taut stomach, which tapered into a V-shape into his chiseled pelvic area.

"How was the rest of the party?" Lo asked.

KC noticed the happy trail below Lo's navel that had previously escaped her glance. The light tuft of fur peeked out from the tied waistband of his pants.

"Hello?" Lo waited for a response.

KC stopped staring. Since she hadn't heard the question, she changed the conversation. "Your application was approved, and so was my request for a staff budget. Thank you."

"Thank you! We did it! We're opening in 'Ohana Circle!" he yelled to the rest of the Center.

No one else was there.

A lone dust ball rolled across the studio floor.

"I'll tell Vin later." Lo clapped his hands together. "We should celebrate. Let's go to lunch."

KC checked her phone. "It's 10:30."

"Then brunch. We'll talk about business."

"I could eat. How about Valeria Wu's?"

"Let's go!" Lo headed for the door in his bare feet.

"*Un momentito, chico*. Although I'm enjoying the view," KC blinked at Lo's damp chest, "and I wouldn't call Kapualani Ranch a business formal type of place, most restaurants require a shirt and shoes for service."

Lo pulled both items out of a nearby cubby, tugged a polo over his head, and held open the door for KC. "Your loss."

22. The big one.
Tue morning, Oct 21, 2014

"Why dance?"

"Why not?"

At a booth next to the front window of the restaurant, with a scant number of brunchers, KC dug into her loco moco plate. "These weren't on the Valeria Wu's menu in Reubenville."

"Good, no? I grew up on these in small kid time," Lo said.

"Why aren't you eating it now, in big adult time?"

"Too much meat." Lo continued munching his vegan antipasto salad and fried rice. "I love dance. And Taekwondo and Karate and Muay Thai. I studied some Capoeira during university. I like moving around, so I learned how to get paid for it."

"And now you teach?"

"Mostly I manage other instructors; some of the best in the Homestead network. I'm good at martial arts, I'm really good at dance, but I'm not great."

"You looked great to me at the luau."

Lo looked pleased. "Did I?"

KC felt her cheeks warm. "You put on a good performance."

"Thank you. Why business development?"

"Me?"

"Did you grow up dreaming of wearing a suit to work every day?"

"It was my second choice after astronaut," KC replied. "And ballerina. Three-season wool is more forgiving than a leotard and tights."

"As someone who has worn all of those, I beg to differ."

"Business was a practical choice. Even though I did okay in Physics, and my mother was thrilled about the possibility of my becoming the first Hispanic astronaut from Southern California whom she knew personally, I didn't want to jump through all the hoops to apply to NASA."

"Too much work?" Lo asked.

"It's like having to become a pilot to fly in an airplane. I just wanted someone to take me to the moon or to Mars or another galaxy. Ironically, after the evacuation, I could have..." KC trailed off.

She stared out the picture window, which overlooked the west end of Big Beach. Tourists strolled along the Waterfront past a variety of booths offering activities and attractions. KC's right hand hovered over her plate, her fingers clenched around her fork, brown gravy dripping off the fried egg still stuck on the tongs.

"Are you okay?"

KC turned to Lo, who look frightened.

"I'm fine. Why?"

"You haven't moved for two full minutes."

KC looked at her hand, still poised in the air. She lowered her hand and set her fork on her plate. "I'm working on that."

...

"I like business brunch," KC said, as she and Lo stood up from the booth, finished with their meal.

"I have good ideas," Lo said. "See how the place is filling up now? We got here at a good time."

The two headed for the exit on the other side of Valeria Wu's.

"Thanks again for suggesting this." KC maneuvered around the other diners.

"Thanks for pushing my application through."

KC shook her head as they walked past the bar. "I didn't exert any undue influence. I submit the documents as I receive the requests."

"Still, it doesn't hurt to have connections to Homestead Headquarters greasing the—"

The ground shook under KC and Lo's feet, moving the chairs across the floor.

The multicolored bottles lining the bar shelves started clinking against each other.

The glass mugs hanging overhead followed suit. One hit the granite countertop with a smash.

Someone in the kitchen screamed.

"Get down." KC grabbed Lo and pulled him under an empty table. They huddled together until the earthquake was over.

Once the shaking stopped, the restaurant staff and patrons emerged from their safety spaces.

KC stood up to look through the intact windows. Outside the restaurant, people were scared, but there was no visible damage.

KC heard a television turn on inside the restaurant. A local news report played on the bar TV. "There have been no injuries reported and no structural damage suspected, since all the buildings on the island are earthquake reinforced," the reporter stated. "There has been no tsunami watch issued."

Lo dusted the ceiling debris off of KC's shoulder. "I should call the middle school to see if my kids are okay."

KC continued watching the reporter on the broadcast. "Subways are fine. Helicopter crews are reporting that the back roads are fine."

"I got a text from my mother. She and my father are fine, but they haven't heard from the girls." Lo kept dialing on his phone. "The circuits are busy."

"Everyone's probably calling everyone else," KC told him. "Knowing how these structures are reinforced, the school should be secure, but keep trying."

The reporter on the screen received an update. "An avalanche on the mountain slope dividing Kapualani Ranch from 'Ohana Circle. The main road joining the two towns is blocked with falling rocks. Traffic is jammed. And an ambulance from 'Ohana Circle traveling to the hospital in Kapualani Ranch is stuck on the other side of the divide with a woman from the 'Ohana Circle School in labor."

"I can't get through!" Lo shouted.

KC guided him outside. "I have an idea."

23. On the road.
Tue afternoon, Oct 21, 2014

"How far is the school from here?"

Lo followed KC out to the sidewalk. "From here on the Waterfront, 10 to 15 minutes."

"By bus?" KC asked.

Lo looked at the streets jammed with large transport vehicles. "The subway doesn't go up hills."

"Oh, that's right," KC sulked. "There goes my idea."

The traffic lights blinked erratically, further complicating the transit situation.

"Walking is the only option right now," Lo said. "Why didn't I buy Nala that phone when she asked for it?"

"I would walk with you, although I might slow you down. I'm not in performing artist shape."

"Even if we go slower, I'll be calmer with you next to me."

KC turned to the tourist-targeted kiosks stationed along Big Beach. "I'll come along. But let's go quicker."

...

"Put it on."

"My head's too big."

Standing in front of their matching rental mopeds, KC adjusted the bright orange helmet resting on Lo's skull. "You had it backward."

Lo's hands shook as he snapped the clasp around his chin. "Ready."

With her dark curls banded in a low ponytail under her neon pink helmet, KC mounted her bike. She turned the key, checked the foot traffic around her, and was about to steer toward the road when—

"I can't get this engine to turn on." Too frazzled about his children to concentrate, Lo toppled onto the pavement. "I just need to get there. Why is my moped not working?"

KC walked her electric bike over to Lo. She pulled him to a standing position. "Hop on."

...

"Watch out for that tree!"

"Where?"

"Right there!"

Lo pointed to the side of the road as KC steered their bike past a fallen twig.

KC continued traversing the side streets of Kapualani Ranch with Lo's directions, dodging obstacles big and small, real and perceived. The vehicle, like the others on the road, floated by, generating less noise than a hybrid car. "I'm surprised you don't have your own moped or motorcycle," KC shouted.

"You don't have to yell. I'm sitting right behind you," Lo

said. "The application process would be a hassle, since Homestead wants to keep private passenger vehicles to a minimum. Also, I have two kids."

"You could get a side car. Or two sidecars."

"We usually do fine with the bus and the subway. Except today," Lo sniffled. "I just want them to be okay."

To calm him down, KC asked Lo to tell him about the day his daughters were born. "What was that like?"

"It was ten... almost eleven years ago. Their mother Talon wasn't in labor for long. Snow Belle popped out easily. Nala took her time and didn't cry. She breathed at the nurses with side eye, annoyed at their expectations."

When Lo didn't offer any additional information, KC tried to keep him talking. "What sorts of things do your daughters participate in now?"

"Snow Belle performs in the Pikake Beats summer troupe. She does Hip Hop, Hula, and Tai Chi."

"You're Mini Me. Except for the hair."

"Both of them have much curlier hair than mine. Or Talon's. But Nala straightens hers every day. And she prefers low-key activities."

"Like reading?"

"And silently judging me. I'm afraid of her becoming a mean girl. But Nala's never mean to Snow Belle. Nala acts like the protective big sister, even though she was born four minutes later. Turn left here."

Lo loosened his grip on KC's waist.

KC could feel him relax.

They traveled further away from the urban center of

Kapualani Ranch. The scenery transformed from singular palm trees placed strategically between retail establishments and government buildings to a tropical forest teeming with flora and fauna that had grown accustomed to their human neighbors.

"You're pretty good at this."

"You sound surprised," KC shouted back at Lo, as she kept the bike on their side of the two-lane highway.

"Not because you're a woman!"

"That's convincing."

"Because it's unfamiliar territory."

"I've driven one of these before, when the Associates traveled to Rome last year. More powerful than they look. I called them our Italian Stallions. Get it?"

"I don't."

"And these roads have fewer potholes than I grew with up in California. So—"

"There it is." Lo pointed at the vine-encrusted arch up ahead of them, with the words "A. Zanzibar Middle School" carved at the top of the hulking wood structure.

As they rode up the jungle hills to the school's main campus, KC heard the school bell ring. She saw hordes of adolescents exit their otherwise undisturbed classrooms en route to their next period location.

"It's like nothing happened at all," KC said.

"I'll believe that when I see my children," Lo replied. "You can park over there."

They pulled up to the open gate outside the school office, left the moped in the lot, and found a few other parents waiting near the entrance.

Lo felt his phone ringing in his pocket. "Of course now it's working. Hello, Mom? I just got to the school."

KC crossed her arms, wondering what she was supposed to do next as a nonparent in this situation.

Then she heard a familiar voice.

"How awkward to have your parents show up at your school." It was Nala, holding court over Snow Belle and their bevy of friends walking near the gate. She pointed at the worried adults searching for their children.

"Totally," her friends lemminged.

"Is it that bad?" Snow Belle asked her sister.

"I love Dad, but I need my space, right?" Nala giggled.

"Right?" The other girls echoed.

Snow Belle rolled her eyes. Then turned to the gate. Through the links, she saw KC nudging her father, who wouldn't get off the phone. "Dad?"

Lo saw his offspring a few feet away. "Snow Belle?" He ran over to the group.

Snow Belle ran toward him and leaped into her father's arms for a hug.

Lo held his daughter tight, kissing the top of her head, her black ringlets shaved into a low fade.

Nala adopted a blank face, pretending she was bored by the situation.

Then she saw KC.

24. And you are?
Tue afternoon, Oct 21, 2014

"What are you doing here?"

"Making sure you're okay," Lo replied to Nala, as he set Snow Bell onto the paved path. He moved to hug his other daughter.

Nala moved back, avoiding her father's arms. "I meant her." She scrunched her nose in the direction of KC.

"Who's that, Dad?" Snow Belle asked.

"This is KC. Nala, you met her on Saturday. At the Community Center."

Nala shook her head.

"Outside the premiere party," Lo pressed. "For the fantenovela?"

Nala provided no evidence that she recalled those events.

Snow Belle walked to KC. "Hi."

KC shook her hand. "You're Snow Belle, right? Nice to meet you."

Snow Belle beamed.

"Nala, what's wrong?" Lo asked.

"Nothing. I'm going to class."

"Don't you have lunch now?"

Nala looked around at the other students eating at picnic tables around the verdant campus. "Whatever." She skulked off with her friends scurrying behind her.

Lo stood dejected in his daughter's moody wake.

Snow Belle tugged on her father's shirt. "Can I have another hug?"

Lo recovered. "Sure, Snow." He picked her up and put her down. "I'll see you after school."

Snow Belle took off after her sister.

Lo turned to KC, who had silently witnessed the whole ordeal. "Did I mention they're identical?"

"No way."

"Nature versus nurture." Lo walked toward the parking lot through the throng of other fretful guardians. "They're fine. I overreacted."

KC patted him on the back. "My parents embarrassed me throughout my childhood, and look how I turned out. I'm wearing a designer suit in the jungle. Also, natural disaster. You had an appropriate reaction."

"I'm sorry about all this," Lo said. "I'm keeping you from your job."

"This was an adventure!"

"Or a course on how not to be a parent."

"Want to make it up to me?"

Lo strapped on his helmet. "Sure."

KC tossed him the keys. "Drive me back to civilization."

25. Rabble roused.
Thu night, Oct 23, 2014

"And that's why our towns are stronger together."

"What does that even mean?!"

Under the fluorescent overhead lights of the stuffed Meeting Room B in the Big Beach Community Center complex, the Mayor shrank from the crowd of angry citizens. He nervously gathered his notecards. "I'm off to another engagement, but I hear your concerns. Shira?"

The Mayor ceded the podium and lumbered away from the front of the room to undecipherable shouts. "Remember," he said, as he headed for the exit, "my office is always open."

The doors slammed shut behind him.

Shira left her seat next to KC and Swan's family. She stepped up to the front, facing the motley crew representing the variety of people who called 'Ohana Circle their home. "What an amazing turnout tonight."

"Didn't expect all of us to show up, did you?" A woman in a straw hat yelled from her folding chair.

"Hitchcock," Shira replied, "I am pleasantly surprised this town hall meeting has yielded such interest."

Next to Hitchcock, another woman with a burgeoning belly stood up to respond, "We don't even get a hall in our own town for us to meet in."

"Scully, we are in your town," Shira said. "This is the 'Ohana Circle side of Big Beach."

"But we don't have our own space," A disheveled man shouted from the second row. "Crammed us into this closet."

"Harlan, the other rooms were already reserved."

"No to the status quo!" A man in the back yelled.

"No justice, no peace!" Another person volunteered.

"Yes, we can!"

"Love, not hate, makes our island great!" Snow Belle cheered from her seat between her sister and father.

Shira waved her hands to acknowledge the many concerns of the people in the room. "Let's go one at a time. Yes, Harlan, go on."

He rose to speak. "We need our own resources in 'Ohana Circle. We are the fastest growing town on the island."

"There are only two towns on the island," the distinguished woman sitting next to him said.

Harlan gestured to the woman. "Miss Lani, as many of you know, her daughter was the one who had to give birth in that ambulance."

"She gave birth at the hospital," Miss Lani clarified.

Harlan continued, "What if she hadn't gotten to a doctor in time?"

"There was a doctor in the ambulance."

"Then Miss Lani would never have met her first grandchild."

"It's my second grandchild."

"Miss Lani would never see that baby take her first step."

"She's two days old."

"That's why we need our own hospital in 'Ohana Circle, so her daughter can rest and recover in her own town."

"She's resting in her own home," Miss Lani corrected. "She was released yesterday."

Shira jumped in. "Harlan, you've made... points. To assess what the town needs, I propose we form a committee."

The hundreds of residents in the humid room loudly agreed.

Pleased with their gusto, Shira clapped her hands. "Who would like to volunteer?"

Crickets.

She zeroed in on the most vocal citizen. "Harlan?"

Harlan reached for his pocket. "I've got a fake phone call. Hello?" He walked out of the room.

Miss Lani raised her hand. "I'll head the committee."

The room applauded.

"Thank you, Miss Lani! I'll send you the details," Shira said.

Miss Lani nodded. "And I'll let my husband know when he returns from his fake phone call."

Shira turned back to the group. "We also need

someone with urban planning experience. Someone involved with the expansion of communities in new areas. Swan? KC?"

KC sat up at attention.

Swan had a dubious look on her face. "How much time will this committee take away from our family and loved ones?"

Shira shrugged. "Maybe two hours a week?"

"Because some people," Swan said, "have already expressed concerned that other people don't spend enough time with them. And now some people want other people to add another commitment to their schedule?"

Hitchcock whispered to Scully, "Which people?"

Scully shrugged.

Shira looked stricken.

KC leaped up. "I'll do it. I don't have any family or loved ones."

Shalom frowned at her.

"No, I love you," KC assured

Shalom uncrossed her arms, pleased.

Shira cleared her throat. "Thank you, KC. We also need committee members with roots in the community, two or three generations on the island, and a new generation of their own."

On the other side of the room, sitting with his family, Lo shifted in his folding chair.

"We need a business owner who wants to add to the economy of 'Ohana Circle," Shira said. "Someone whose company has brought pride and prestige to Hale Kupua."

Snow Belle nudged her father. "I think she's talking about you, Dad."

"I think so too," Lo said.

Shira braced herself on the podium. "Someone who won't dance around the issues, but will dance on a bea—"

Lo leaned back in his seat and raised his hand in the air. "Shira."

Shira feigned surprise. "Lo?"

"I'll be on the committee."

"Thank you for volunteering."

Lo glanced at KC. "It will be my pleasure."

KC avoided Lo's gaze. "Shira, will there be food at these meetings?"

"Yes," Shira affirmed, "dinner will be provided."

More hands shot up.

KC made a note on her phone. "Should've led with that."

26. What do we want?
Mon night, Oct 27, 2014

"Sweaters for dogs."

"Love it. Put it on the board."

"Hitchcock, I know I said there were no bad ideas, but
—"

"They have them in Kapualani Ranch!"

In Conference Room C at the Big Beach Community
Center, Miss Lani squeezed the dog sweater proposal in
blue marker, between "Hospital" and "Fire Station" on the
white board.

"We have a lot of great suggestions up here for what
the town needs," Miss Lani said, pointing at the board,
which was littered with comparable suggestions from the
score of other members on the committee. "And some
other ones."

"Chocolate fountain," Harlan called out from the back
of the conference table, cookie in hand. "They're real, I've
seen them."

Lo, closer to the front, posed a question. "Even if we
could get all these things, who will pay for them? And
where would we put them? Hale Kupua has crazy
regulations on the construction of new buildings on the
island."

"Yes, for safety and aesthetic purposes," Miss Lani said.

KC, who was seated across from Lo, asked, "What about underground?"

"You mean like stores next to the subway?" Lo asked. "Or the terminals for the Homestead network trains?"

KC laughed. "Not just stores. Expand the community underground."

"Like Naboombu?" KC offered.

Puzzled faces appeared throughout the room.

Lo shrugged.

But Miss Lani raised her eyebrows.

KC realized her misstep.

"You know what?" KC placed her paper napkin over her plate. "We don't need to reinvent the wheel. Homestead keeps records of everything. I'm sure City Hall has the original plans for Kapualani Ranch expanding into 'Ohana Circle."

Miss Lani nodded. "Great idea, KC."

"I'll look for them and bring what I can find to next week's meeting."

"If there are no objections," Miss Lani scanned the room, "then we're adjourned. Thank you all."

Everyone rose from the table and recycled their dinner plates.

Miss Lani placed her hand on KC's shoulder and nodded. "Soon will be the time for your knowledge."

...

As a handful of committee members milled around the

116

exit, KC walked out of the Center into the night air, followed by Lo.

"That was mysterious," Lo caught up with her.

KC continued ambling along the brightly-lit sidewalks of the quiet town. "Are you walking home, or jogging home, burning calories, releasing endorphins, feel that adrenaline rush!"

"I don't exercise nonstop."

"You work out for a living."

"You say that like it's a bad thing."

"I'm stating facts." KC passed a statue of four small girls holding hands as she headed for the San Marino cluster. "What else do you do that doesn't involve physical energy?"

Lo gave this a think. He came up with an answer. "I read."

"Do you?"

"Okay, I've seen movies based on books. But I've thought about reading them."

They kept walking and talking until KC stopped at her building. "This is me."

Lo bowed. "As anticipated, it has been delightful."

"Who's going to walk you home? I know this is practically the safest place on earth..."

"Who's gonna come at me? These hands are classified as lethal weapons." Lo threw punches at an imaginary beanbag. "You don't want none of this."

"That'll keep the no-good-niks away."

"Hey, when do you think you'll look for those plans at City Hall?"

"Maybe tomorrow at lunch?"

Lo had a sad face. "Oh…"

"Or maybe Wednesday at lunch?"

Lo nodded in approval.

"Or Thursday."

Lo shook his head with a growl.

"Wednesday at lunch?" KC repeated.

Lo looked at her expectantly.

"Yes, Wednesday at lunch," KC confirmed. "12:30, depending on the bus, is when I will be at City Hall."

"Coincidentally, I will be in the vicinity of City Hall on Wednesday at 12:30."

"It's five minutes away from your studio."

"I could *not* be in the vicinity."

"Could you be there with sandwiches?" KC asked.

"Veggie wraps?"

"Chicken wraps."

"Chinese chicken salad wraps."

KC shook on it. "Done."

27. Lunch and learn.
Wed afternoon, Oct 29, 2014

"Chicken is delicious."

"And nutritious."

In the verdant garden of the government plaza next to the Kapualani Ranch City Hall, KC and Lo were eating their wraps on a stone bench.

"How are you giving this up for... chick peas?"

Lo swallowed. "It's not every meal. And, my body responds better to vegetable protein than animal protein."

KC thought about this. "Can I ask you a personal question?"

"More personal than asking, 'Does a plant-based diet make your poop less chunky?'"

"You didn't answer."

"Yes. And, yes."

"In the almost four months that I've lived on the island, I haven't seen you date anyone."

"You've been watching me?"

"Although, when you first accosted me at the Welcome Luau on Big Beach like I was Rosa Parks—"

"That's an exaggeration."

"—I thought you an Vin were a couple."

Lo coughed up his wrap. "You thought I was dating Vin?"

"Then she let me know that was not happening."

"Are you trying to ask if I have a girlfriend?"

"Does she live in 'Canada'? Is that why we never see her?"

"I don't have a girlfriend in Canada, or 'Naboombu.'"

"It's a real place. I've been there."

"If you came here four months ago, that's July. Well, of course you did. Then, no. I haven't dated anyone in that time. Or this year."

KC remained mystified. "How?"

"How what?"

"How have you not dated anyone in the past ten months?"

"It's been over a year actually. Almost two since my last real relationship."

"But you're a prime specimen."

"Ew!"

"You're a successful business-ish man who looks like this."

"Like what?"

"You can see yourself in a mirror. I don't understand

why you haven't found a nice woman."

"Have you been talking with my mother? Because you sound just like her."

KC's eyes widened. "Oh, are you..." she whispered to Lo "...in the closet? On the down low?"

"Why would I be in the closet *here*?"

"You're   Pikake   Beats   fans?"

"I'm probably on the Kinsey scale, like every other human on the planet, but I'm a cisgender, heterosexual man."

"Then, what's the deal? Have you run through all the women on Hale Kupua?"

"It is a small island, but no." Lo took KC's cardboard tray and recycled their rubbish. "Let's head inside. I'll explain."

KC and Lo entered the two-story building. After walking through the halls—decorated with photographed portraits of the island's founding families who hailed from countries across the Pacific—the two investigators located the Records Room.

At a heavy table, KC unfurled old blueprints of sites around Hale Kupua that featured staggered growth maps. "This is what we're looking for."

"These are amazing," Lo said. "Look at the detail."

"Don't change the subject."

"Between running the Center and managing the dance troupes. And raising two girls, albeit with the help of my entire family." Lo sat at their table in the corner of the otherwise empty room. "And it's a small island. 40,000 people in Kapualani Ranch. 4,000 in 'Ohana Circle. A few more now. Let's round that up to 50,000 total."

"Okay."

"Maybe 10,000 of them are around my age. Half of them are women."

"Which is 5,000 people!"

"*Un momento, por favor*. We need to eliminate my relatives."

"How many people could that be?"

"I'm a descendant of a founding family. Multiple founding families, actually." Lo angled his head toward the entrance. "We passed a few on the way in here. So I'm related to the majority of the population. Vin's great-grandmother and my great-grandfather were siblings. So we're third cousins?"

"Huh!"

"Especially in 'Ohana Circle, they say 'cousins make dozens,' but I'm not about that inbred life. So that leaves 100 women on Hale Kupua I could date. Once you eliminate the ones who are either married, in a relationship, not into men. Some combination; it's slim pickings."

KC picked up the papers and carried them to the copy room. "Have you dated all of those women?"

"Here's where the story takes a turn for the supernatural. Superstitious? The ones who are left think I am cursed."

"Whyyy?"

"Every girl, or *woman*—"

"Thank you."

"—I've been with has left the island. Everyone I dated in high school, middle school, my kids' mother, all gone."

"How did you drive them away?"

"It wasn't all me! I wasn't even dating most of them when they left. It's a coincidence that has become a cautionary folktale that kids here tell around the campfire."

KC lowered her voice. "'And, children, he never knew the love of a good woman again.'"

"It's not funny."

"Yeah, it is. How can you break the curse?"

"It's not a real curse! It's a story a bunch of gossipy islanders made up about me because they were bored. Possibly, if the next person I dated didn't leave the island, for the rest of her life, then the curse would be over."

"What if she stayed on the island for the rest of her life, but she stopped dating you?"

"I don't know. I'd have to ask."

KC picked up their copies. "Or, what if one of your old girlfriends came back to the island, didn't date you, but outlived you?"

"Then, in that scenario, I would be dead."

KC guided Lo to the exit, past the pictures of his ancestors. "But would you still be cursed?"

Outside in the bright courtyard, KC held their copies of the blueprints under her arm.

"What about you?" Lo asked.

"Me?"

"I haven't seen you dating anyone since Alvester."

"We *just* broke up."

"It's been four weeks."

"You've been counting?"

"So, I'm guessing you don't have plans for Halloween?"

"I do have plans," KC said. "Not during the day on Friday. But that night, my book club—my book club, I have a book club. We're going to a throwback costume party downtown. I'm deciding between bellbottoms, leg warmers, and baby tees, but my outfit will be fabulous. What are you doing?"

"I'm dressing as Sherlock Holmes. No, Snow Belle told me I'm the Great Mouse Detective. And I'm chaperoning the dance at their school."

"Nala must be thrilled."

"She hates me—her words—and she will not talk to me all night."

"The life of a dad."

"I'll see you on Monday then?"

"You're not going to the fantenovela watch party on Saturday?"

"Nala's going to her friend's birthday bash. My 10-year-old has plans for Saturday night, and I don't. Nice!"

"You don't watch fantenovelas on your own?"

"She got me into them. But there's no reason I can't watch them by myself as a man. I will be at that watch party Saturday night. Will you be there?"

"I will," KC said, with confidence. "It's a da—I will see you there."

28. All hollow.
Fri night, Oct 31, 2014

"A money fountain with a fish scale?"

"No, it fits with the party's 80s and 90s theme."

In the downtown pub, which was dripping with black and orange decorations for the holiday and pulsing with New Jack Swing melodies over the sound system, KC examined Vin's costume one more time. "I give up."

"I'm a balanced budget. And you're a..." Vin poked the silver 1814 badge on KC's black jacket that mirrored the one on KC's black baseball cap, "...mercenary soldier?"

KC spun on her barstool. "Rhythm Nation? 1814?"

"Ohhh." Vin sipped her bright green cocktail in a plastic jack-o-lantern-shaped novelty mug. "Janet. Right."

"Ding! *Scream 2!*" Eleanor shouted from a nearby table.

"You can ding the bell in front of us," Maxine, wearing a scarf and beret, reminded her. "You don't have to say, 'ding.'"

"I want to make sure the host can hear me."

"We all hear you," Scully, who was dressed as a gumball machine, replied into her microphone.

"Did you get our points?" Eleanor asked.

Hitchcock, attired in Rainbow Brite gear from yellow wig to striped knee boots, updated the score on the trivia screen.

"The last question moved you and Maxine into the lead by 10 points, ahead of Steve and Ben."

From their spectator seats, KC and Vin continued watching the competition unfold in front of them.

At the table next to Eleanor, the man in the yellow hat waved at Hitchcock. "Do we get points for our throwback costumes?"

"What are you, Steve," Eleanor sneered in her own pinstriped suit and fedora, "the guy from Curious George? Is Ben your monkey?"

"I'm Chewbacca," Ben retorted.

"And I'm Dick Tracy," Steve said.

"Doesn't count. That's a comic from the 1930s," Eleanor said.

"It's a movie from the 1990s," Steve corrected. "Who are you two? Al Capone and his moll?"

"We're Bonnie and Clyde," Maxine declared.

"Speaking of the 1930s," Ben said.

"They're timeless," Eleanor said. "And, we look awesome."

"Says who?" Steve taunted.

Scully tapped on her microphone. "Can we get back to the game, please?"

"Yes, we're ready," Maxine said.

"For ten points!" Scully read from the screen in front of her. "No strangers to the horror genre, this real-life mother and daughter duo teamed up for a 1998 sequel that threatened to axe a holiday franchise."

As the front door of the establishment swung open, the bells hanging in the middle jangled, announcing the arrival of additional guests to the party.

"Oh my gosh." KC pulled her cap further down her forehead.

"Do you know the answer?" Vin asked. "Because I've almost got it."

KC sneaked a glance behind her. "I'll be right back."

KC darted toward the painted arrow pointing to the restrooms. She hid behind a steel pillar.

Vin looked around for what KC was hiding from.

In walked Alvester, wearing tan coveralls, with black work boots and elbow pads. He was holding hands with a sophisticated woman dressed in a black leather feline ensemble.

KC remained in her secret spot, observing Alvester and his date greet the other partygoers, including Ben and Steve, who had come from behind to tie Eleanor and Maxine for the top spot. Alvester was still hovering around the area of KC's vacated stool. Apparently, he knew everyone at the event, and they had all decide her empty seat was the perfect location to congregate.

KC slinked past a zombie, a zombie, and another zombie, and entered the Women's room to wait out the situation. As she leaned on one of the porcelain sinks, her hip pocket buzzed. KC pulled out her phone to find a photo of an old tyme detective bearing a monocle and a magnifying glass.

"Taken by Snow Belle," KC read the accompanying caption from Lo, "the only daughter of mine who is talking to me."

KC typed on the keypad, "Nice hat, Sherlock." She took a selfie and included a message. "Hiding in the loo for reasons."

After she pressed Send, KC heard a commotion outside the door. She headed back to the party via the skeleton-laden hallway lit with dim red bulbs and bumped face first into another patron.

"Sorry," KC said to the other woman. "It's so dark in here."

It was Alvester's date.

KC stood there, stunned.

"With half the people at this party dressed in black," the woman said, "you think they'd turn on a light."

KC remained immobile, breathing with her mouth open.

The woman pointed at KC's outfit. "Nice. Miss Jackson, if you're nasty."

KC closed her mouth.

The woman pointed at her own costume. "Catwoman. Michelle Pfeiffer, not Halle Berry."

"Or Eartha Kitt," KC offered.

The woman laughed. "Right? Well, Happy Halloween." She disappeared into the restroom.

KC heard cheers coming from the bar and followed the sounds. She scanned the area for Alvester's face, didn't see him anywhere, and reclaimed her seat.

"You came back just in time," Vin told her. "It's neck and neck, and they're down to the last question."

"What 1992 film," Scully read, "whose titular character shares a moniker with the Sammy Davis Jr.—?"

"Candyman!" Eleanor and Steve yelled simultaneously, as they slammed on their respective bells.

Hitchcock held up her hand. "Since you both answered correc—"

"Candyman! Candyman! Candyman!" The two competitors repeated.

"Please don't say it again," Scully requested.

"Who gets the points?" Eleanor demanded.

"As I was saying," Hitchcock continued, "Since you both —"

"I dinged first," Steve insisted.

"We get the points, we win," Ben said.

"Pipe down, Chachi," Eleanor said.

"It's Chewy." Steve rose from his stool. "Besides, we know you cheated."

"You saying we didn't know the answers?" Eleanor asked Steve.

"Sistah, no need. Obvious."

Eleanor removed her earrings. "You want to scrap?"

"Not again," Vin sighed to KC.

Ben called someone over to help him talk his trivia partner down.

"I don't beef with wahines," Steve said.

"That's not what I heard," Maxine said.

"Maxine, you're not helping," Vin called out.

"Let's settle this on the scoreboard," Ben proposed, with his palm pressed on Steve's shoulder. "Sudden-death tiebreaker."

Hitchcock clapped her hands. "That's what I've been trying to—"

"Or we can take this outside." Eleanor unbuckled her gaudy watch.

Steve wriggled away from Ben. He stepped into Eleanor's space. "Don't start something you can't finish."

KC watched as Alvester appeared from the shadows. He and Ben edged between the two combatants.

"Steve, you're finished here." With Ben's help, Alvester led an intractable Steve toward the exit.

"Why me?" Steve whined, resisting his comrades' nudges. "She started it."

Eleanor made a face at him.

Ben kept pushing. "Do you really want to battle over a gift card to the Taco Hole?"

"Or do you want to get some fresh air and avoid your third drunk and disorderly arrest this year?" Alvester asked.

"I'm not drunk," Steve grouched. "Fine, let's go."

Alvester turned to look in KC's direction. "I'll be right back."

Before KC could open her mouth to speak, she heard a voice from behind her.

"Okay, Al," his date replied.

"Al?" Vin whispered to KC.

Ben helped shepherd his buddy around Hitchcock and Scully. "Sorry for the disturbance."

"Just another Hale Kapua holiday," Hitchcock remarked.

As the three men passed the other contestants' tables, Alvester told Steve, "Say goodnight to your sister."

"Good night, Eleanor."

She kissed Steve on his cheek. "See you at church on Sunday. Oh, and Ben?" Eleanor cocked her head toward her brother's friend. "We win."

29. What had happened was.
Sat morning, Nov 01, 2014

"Then I carried my gift bag of fun-size treats out the back, rode a bus back to my apartment, and fell asleep on my bed."

KC sat on her therapist's couch, proud of surviving the previous night. "All in all, I had a good Friday. Even though I didn't actually speak to Alvester. Not that I would've known what to say. 'Sorry for breaking your heart'?"

KC glowered. "Although he got right back on that horse again with swiftness. Like the proverb says, men don't heal; they ho. I don't know which book of the Bible that's in, and his date wasn't... she seemed respectable, from what little I gathered. Why do I care?

"ANYWAY," KC continued, "everything else is fine. Work is good. I've been meeting with business executives in 'Ohana Circle. At first they were scared I was going to change a bunch of stuff, but when I explained I'm here to listen and help, they chilled out and brought me food. Most of them are farmers. They feed the island, but they don't have the representation in the local government that they deserve. Which I brought up at the committee meeting that I mentioned earlier."

KC sat up straighter. "I'm getting involved! I went to Vin's yoga class this morning. She was annoyingly chipper, while I was huffing and puffing through the sun salutations. And I read books now, because I'm in a book club. And I've interacted with members of the book club at multiple events over a period of time, so that's healthy. Maybe I have new friends?

"See, I'm fine," KC said. "Better than I was, at least. I think that's everything."

KC looked toward the translucent white curtains diffusing the sunbeams through the window. "Has anything else affected my life lately?" KC contemplated her question.

A buzz sounded on KC's hip.

KC clicked off her phone and returned it to her pocket.

"Nope."

30. Do you hear what I hear?
Sat night, Nov 01, 2014

"Yes, I'm sure."

"No one at all?"

"If they had, I would know." KC lowered her voice as the lights dimmed in Conference Room D at the Big Beach Community Center. "The trivia area was right in front of me. No one threw a punch."

In the second row of seats in the sparsely populated space, Lo tilted his head toward KC who was sitting next to him.

"Must've been an altercation at another nostalgia party."

The latest episode in the *Mirage of the Mines* saga played on the projector screen.

KC whispered to Lo. "Speaking of nostalgia—"

"Shh!" Scully, who was stuffing her gullet with kettle corn next to Hitchcock, turned around to quiet KC.

KC took her purse and Lo to sit on the floor in the back of the room. They settled next to the sliding glass doors, 20 feet away from the nearest fantenovela watcher, of which there were few.

KC continued her whisper. "How was your return to middle school?"

Lo crossed his legs on the bamboo tiles. "More fun than I thought it would be. I knew maybe half the songs? But most of the kids weren't dancing. They were playing candy-related pranks on each other."

In the dark, Lo and KC quietly observed the romance between the characters unfold before their eyes.

As the plot shifted from the discovery of the body to a chase scene, Lo inquired of KC, "What were the reasons you were hiding?"

"When was this?"

"Last night," Lo said, facing the screen, "when you took the picture in the bathroom mirror."

"Yes, I do recall. I didn't want to add fuel to my own rumor fire. Back to you. What tricks and treats did you create after the dance?"

Lo stretched his right tricep, then the left one, behind his head. "None. I chaperoned the students from 'Ohana Circle on the school bus back home, then I went to sleep. Snow Belle and Nala stayed up watching *Paranormal Activity*."

"I expected a more raucous Friday excursion from a guy like you."

"I can't party like I used to. I didn't think I'd wear out so quickly until my 30s."

"Wait, what?"

"Yeah, you're right. I turn 30 next year, which explains it."

"Next year?" KC narrowed her eyes at him. "You're 29."

"28. I'll be 29 in December."

"Whaaa? I thought you were..."

"How old are you?"

"Never ask a lady her age. 34."

"That's six years difference. You were out here dating Grandpa Moses—"

Hitchcock and Scully both swiveled in their seats. "Shh!"

KC ushered Lo outside to the porch overlooking the sand and surf of Big Beach. She shut the sliding glass doors behind them.

"You were 18?"

"When the twins were born? Yeah."

"And then you built all this in less than 10 years?"

"It wasn't easy. And I had help."

"What have I done with my life?" KC leaned on the porch rail. She gazed at the waves crashing on the shore in front of her.

"We're back to you now?

"18? I couldn't have done it."

"I seriously have my entire family raising my children. I'm not a superhero. I'm a parent."

"I have zero dependents: Where's my world-renowned dance company?"

"Were you planning on opening before or after you and your Associate friends created sustainable communities from scratch in four different countries for over 100,000 people?"

"200,000. But it got shut down by the government."

"Temporarily. It will come back. No one keeps Homestead down for long. I couldn't have done what you did."

"You would've been a great Associate. You're smart and resourceful, and limber—"

"I meant, leaving everything you know behind to come here. I, we, the people who grew up in Homestead take it for granted. I know I did until I left for college. But if life outside is all you know, then outside is home, no matter how dreadful."

"I wanted to go back." KC shook her head. "No, I didn't. When we learned the evacuation was coming, I thought it would be easier to go back. I had it all planned out. But I realized I had changed. I had developed higher expectations for my life, for other people, for my world. I couldn't go back to living in the patriarchy. So, Swan said, 'You're coming with me—and my daughter and my father and my ex-husband—to 'Ohana Circle,' and here I am."

"''Ohana means family. Family means no one gets left behind or forgotten.'"

"Thanks, Lilo."

"Even though it's under horrific circumstances, I'm glad you're here."

"Why?"

"Because I like you." Lo put his arm around KC's shoulders and squeezed "There are a thousand specific reasons I could name."

"A thousand?"

Lo counted on his fingers. "Okay, four. But they're

important."

"I can think of more than four reasons you should like me."

"I'm crossing 'humble' off the list. Now it's down to three."

"If only I could name three reasons I like you. It's a mystery!"

Scully knocked on the glass from inside the room. She mashed her puffy belly against the door and shushed KC and Lo once again.

"The door's soundproof," Lo cogitated. "I can't believe she teaches geniuses for a living."

"Where?"

"At 'Ohana Circle. The 'Ohana Circle School. It's the boarding school for gifted teenagers at the east end of the island. Scully teaches them math. She was in my sister and older cousin's year in school. They told me Scully knew every answer to every question, but she always wore pajamas to class because she forgot to change in the morning. Now she's allowed to inflict her knowledge upon minors."

"Reminds me of my friend Luz. Total baby genius, crazy math prodigy, but can't figure out adulting."

"Friend from university?"

"One of the Associates," KC said. "Moved to an undisclosed location. Never shushed me. I miss her."

Lo rubbed KC's shoulder. "Are you hungry?"

"Always. What do you have in mind?"

"I would like to inflict my vegan cooking on you, but my

Mom and Dad are watching Snow Belle at my place."

"Are you afraid they'll eat all the food?

"I didn't think you'd... You want to hang out with my family?"

"Unless you think it would be weird."

"I think it's awesome." He typed on his phone. "I'll let them know we're coming."

They ambled from the porch across the sand to the bus stop.

"Meeting your parents. Big development. What's next, calling the caterer?"

"Don't give my mother any ideas."

31. Family matters.
Sat night, Nov 01, 2014

Lo's mother opened the apartment door before Lo could enter the key in the lock.

"KC, these are my parents," Lo said.

"Ms. Hobbs, right?" KC asked.

"Mom, this is KC."

Lo's mother hugged KC. "Yes! We've heard so much about you."

"Mom!"

Snow Belle walked over to the entrance. "Dad says you're going to save our town."

"I will certainly try." KC turned to Lo. "Where should I sit?"

"Next to me!" Snow Belle pulled KC to the couch.

"Nice to meet you, KC." Lo's father waved from the kitchen, where he was tending to bubbling pots on the stove.

"You too, Mr. Gambon."

"Dad, I said I was going to cook."

"I know. That's why I'm making this, so the rest of us have something to eat.

...

"And then Marlowe said, 'That's my binky!'"

Everyone at the bounteous dining table laughed, except for Lo.

"Good story, Tutu," Snow Belle said to her grandmother.

Lo's father reached into his pocket. "Let me see if I have a picture of him in the tub."

"Dad!"

The front door swung open.

Nala entered, saw KC, and frowned.

Lo got up to give Nala a hug. "How was the party?

Nala didn't hug him back. "What's she doing here?"

"Nala, don't be rude," Lo's mother said.

"We have a guest," Lo's father said. "Use your manners."

Nala dropped her bag and walked over to KC to shake her hand. "Good evening, Miss KC. Are you sleeping with my father?"

Lo stormed over to his daughter. "That is not appropriate! Go get ready for bed!"

"What about Snow Belle?" Nala asked.

"You too, Snow Belle."

"I didn't do anything!" she yelled at her father.

"Both of you go." Lo pointed at the hallway. "Now!"

Nala walked to her room. "Wear a condom!"

"Nala!" her grandfather admonished.

Snow Belle tailed her sister out of the living room. "Why are you like this?"

Lo and his parents avoided KC's eyes.

"I'm sorry about that," Lo said. "I don't know what got into her."

KC stood up from the table. "Thank you for dinner. Ms. Hobbs, Mr. Gambon, it was so nice to meet you."

Lo's parents both gave KC hugs.

"We hope to see you again soon," Mr. Gambon said.

Ms. Hobbs said to her son, "Yes, soon, Marlowe."

Lo pushed in his chair. "I'll walk you out."

KC stepped around Nala's bag sitting in front of the door. "I'll be fine."

Lo dashed after her. "Wait!"

32. We're here.
Sat night, Nov 01, 2014

KC and Lo stood in silence at the bus stop outside of the Windhoek cluster.

KC opened her mouth to speak. Then she closed it.

"What were you going to say?" Lo asked.

"I have no idea. That's why I closed my mouth."

"I'm sorry. Again! Nala's probably up there getting yelled at by both grandparents, if that's any consolation."

"She knows how to get your attention."

"She's usually the quiet one."

"She's scared."

"Scared of what? Dinner?

The bus arrived.

KC climbed on. Lo followed her up the step, texting before he sat down on the padded bench.

The bus departed.

KC wondered why Lo was seated next to her. "Shouldn't you be at home?"

"The two adults who raised me have it under control. Scared of what?"

"I don't know what this," she gestured between them, "is yet, but when's the last time you brought someone to your house?"

"We usually hang out at my parents' place. It's bigger, because it's next to the farm."

"Have you brought anyone there who wasn't related to you?"

"The dancers from the traveling troupes at the Center. Although most of them are fourth cousins or closer."

"Have you brought any nonemployees to the farm?"

"There was a dog once. Mittens. But we put her owner on the payroll."

"*Mijo*, your daughter doesn't want a new mother!"

They sat still in the mostly empty bus, which rolled on to the next destination.

KC crossed her arms. "I know that wasn't your intention, and I didn't plan on having this conversation ever, much less so quickly. But that's what's happening."

Lo ruminated on KC's proclamation.

The bus slowed down at KC's stop.

"That was fast," Lo said.

The two of them exited the vehicle and walked to KC's building as the bus drove away, leaving them alone in the dark.

"Hypothetically," Lo said, "since we're here, do you want to be a mother, or a stepmother?"

"Non-hypothetically, yes. That's why I broke up with

Alvester."

"I heard it was because the ring was too small."

"There was no ring! Since we're here, do you want to have more children?"

"Yes. It's hard to do without a uterus though."

"Is that all you want? A womb?"

"I didn't realize I wanted anything. Until now. I blame you."

"What *do* you want?" KC asked.

"What do *you* want?" Lo replied.

"I'm trying to figure that out. That's why I have a therapist. She wants me to ask more questions each time I enter something new."

"Ask me anything."

"What do you want in your next relationship?"

Lo took her hands. "I want my next relationship to be with you."

"What else?"

"I want your next relationship to be with me."

KC rolled her eyes.

"I'm being honest!" Lo avowed. "I don't know what else to say."

"What are you doing tomorrow?"

"Tomorrow's Sunday, my day of rest. I make time to enjoy nature, commune with the earth, and appreciate the bounty that the land and sea have provided to us."

"How spiritual. Are you planting trees at the farm?"

"No, I'm surfing at Big Beach. Eating some poke. It's also my cheat day."

"In between catching a wave and cramming raw fish into your face, can you think about your needs and expectations and deal breakers?"

"So touchy-feely."

"Do it while you're communing with the earth. And write it down."

"You're giving me a homework assignment?"

"I will do one too," KC said. "Call me when you're done, and we'll compare."

"It sounds like a lot of work."

KC took a step back. "Well, then, goodnight." She shook his hand. "It's been real."

She walked away from Lo, entered the building, and headed for the elevator.

KC pushed the button.

Inside the elevator car, a melody chimed from KC's phone.

"Hello?"

"I'll have it done by noon."

33. Import/export business.
Sun morning, Nov 02, 2014.

"I seem what?"

"Happy! You seem happy."

KC pushed her cart alongside Swan's down the aisles of the 'Ono Market. "Are *you* happy?"

Swan dragged a gallon of milk into her top basket. "I am. I wasn't sure how everyone would adjust, but it's good. I like seeing Shira in person on a regular basis. I like working at the same office in the same building at the same hospital every weekday and spending every weekend in the same town as my daughter."

KC pawed through the scant number of orange juice containers in the glass refrigerator. "There's only one bottle left with extra pulp."

"And I like that Shalom can see her father whenever she wants, instead of flying every other holiday to whatever European metropolis Miguelito was traveling to with his team. Which I understand, because I had the same erratic type of schedule when I was playing in the women's league. It's better now."

"It's a peaceful life."

"In a peaceful place," Swan replied.

"Where's my cheese?!"

KC and Swan and the other patrons of the refrigerated aisle watched a woman in a yellow cardigan sift through the cold items on the lit shelf.

"Miss Felice," Swan motored closer to her, "the cheese is right here."

"That's not mine." Stooped over, Miss Felice kept rummaging through the sealed plastic bags. "That's Monterey Jack. That's mild cheddar. That's asadero. That's queso quesadilla. I want the Mexican." Miss Felice looked up at KC. "No offense."

"First of all," KC walked toward the woman, "I'm Mexican American. Chicana, as some of my friends would say. You can call me KC. Second, if you take those four cheeses—"

Miss Felice noticed an item in another woman's cart. "That's my cheese! Cindy, that's your name, right, youngster? Cindy, you took the last one."

"There were more earlier," Cindy knelt down to check the shelf.

"Whatever we have for this section," an 'Ono Market employee interjected as she glided by, "is on the shelves. Next shipment arrives on Monday."

"Monday?!" Miss Felice exclaimed.

"You could come back tomorrow," Swan suggested.

"As I was saying," KC pulled each of the aforementioned cheeses off their respective displays and stacked them in Miss Felice's basket, "if you mix these together, it's the exact same thing. It's not even from Mexico."

Miss Felice frowned at Cindy. "Never enough, with these newcomers."

"I've lived here for ten years," Cindy replied, still searching the shelf for a hidden gem to hand to her antagonist.

"New to me."

"The exact same thing!" KC reiterated to Miss Felice.

Cindy ended her search. She removed the lone package of shredded Mexican 4-cheese from her cart. "Here."

Humility washed over Miss Felice, as she held the gift. "I couldn't."

"You can." Cindy held her hands.

"I shouldn't, as I have shown disrespect to my neighbor."

"You should, as I grant this with the spirit of 'ohana."

Miss Felice and Cindy continued going back and forth. The growing warmth of their palms was melting the shreds into coagulated clumps.

Swan rolled her eyes at KC. "I'm going to get Bran Flakes."

KC focused on the other two women, each trying to be the better person. "I'm going to see how this plays out."

34. Let the record show.
Sun afternoon, Nov 02, 2014.

"What else?"

"That's it."

"You only said two words."

In the center of the park, surrounded by the five two-story apartment buildings that comprised the San Marino cluster, Lo checked his list. "Honesty. Communication."

Protected from the high noon rays, KC looked at him from across the umbrella-shaded picnic table. "And?"

Lo wrote down another word on the creased piece of paper. "Hugs."

KC was not amused.

Lo touched her forearm. "I'm a simple guy. Doesn't take much to make me happy. You're more than enough."

KC had to grin. "Fair point, well made."

Lo ran his fingertips against her skin. "Show me yours."

She slid him a palm-sized pink leather notebook with a slender ribbon marking her place.

Lo read KC's words to himself. "'Fight fair and go to sleep resolved'; I like that." He turned to the next filled page. "'Individuality and teamwork... Togetherness and alone time as well.' That goes for me too."

Lo continued down the small page. "'Third date talk and health screening?' I can do that. 'Acceptance... Patience with my healing'?"

"I'm still processing... everything in my life," KC said with a clear voice, as she adjusted the strap of her tank top. "And since my ship has set down on the shore of Hale Kapua for the next four and a half years, I need someone who wants to enjoy this tropical paradise with me. What are you writing?"

Sniffling, as he wiped away his tears, Lo scribbled furiously on the back of his own list. He regarded his new needs with exhaustion. "I need to sit down."

"You are sitting down."

"Then I need to lie down." Lo got up and walked over to a pair of lounge chairs in the shade of a clump of trees.

KC followed. "These are wet."

"Let me take off my t-shirt to dry these lounge chairs, so we can lie down and think."

KC looked toward her building. "I could get a paper towel."

"No time! Shirt off." He wiped off both seats and squished them close together. Then he spread out his damp apparel on the back to air dry. "Ladies first."

KC rolled her eyes at Lo's chest, bare again. "As I have said before, I'm not complaining but, where I come from, shirts are usually a requirement."

Lo laid back. "You're not from around here."

KC eased herself into the chair next to Lo's.

Lo read his amended thoughts to KC. "After Snow Belle

and Nala go to university, I will probably change careers. I can't dance forever. And by then, I will have spent almost half my life taking care of my kids. So I'll have a brand new start. I need a partner who can handle the uncertainty of my not knowing what I want to do next."

"You only have six years to figure it out, so get cracking."

Lo rotated onto his side to face KC. He rested his head on the heel of his palm. "Did I pass your test?"

"This was not a test," KC replied, mirroring his pose. "It is an ongoing discussion."

"What happens now?"

"The hard part." KC rolled over, stood up, and helped Lo out of his seat. "We go on our first date."

35. I spy.
Sun afternoon, Nov 02, 2014.

"Vegetable, vegetable, not vegetable. Tofu, which is made of beans that grow in the ground?"

"It's okay," Lo assured KC, as they stood in line at the rural food establishment, Kau Kau. "I can figure out what to eat. I heard about this place before from a couple people. And I really can read."

KC pointed to the red and yellow board featuring photographs of available items above the registers. "There are also pictures. Shira took the Associates here on our first visit to Kapualani Ranch. The short rib tacos are so good. Worth the extra charge."

"Korean fusion?" Lo squinted at the middle section of the menu. "I'll get the acai bowl."

"That's so healthy. I thought it was cheat day."

"I'll ask them to put some meat on it," Lo tapped her nose, "just for you."

After placing their orders, KC and Lo searched the crowded shack for a place to sit.

"I wanted to be helpful," KC said, as they waited for a booth to open up. "Because we're dates. We're dating. We are romantic people who care for each other."

"Caring about my nutrition," Lo said. "I should put that on my list."

"Is that you, KC?"

KC saw a small, refined woman standing in front of her. "Mayor Berger?"

Mayor Berger walked toward KC with open arms.

KC started weeping as she bent down for a hug. "I thought you had been relocated to Arco Iris."

"I had, but I made the trip from Argentina."

"I'm so happy to see you. Even though my tears in your hair say otherwise." KC found a napkin and dabbed the drops from Mayor Berger's springy natural black and gray coils.

"And who is this?"

KC introduced Lo and Mayor Berger, who shook hands.

"The dancer," she recalled. "That's how I know your punim."

"It is a beautiful one." Lo winked at them.

"Lo!" The Kau Kau team member bellowed. "Your order is ready."

Lo excused himself and returned to the counter.

"Are you here on vacation?" KC asked Mayor Berger.

"A little work, a little play."

"How's Silver doing?"

"Still in Lake Elmo, but with ants in his pants, as usual. My son never settles..." Something caught Mayor Berger's attention outside the restaurant.

Next to the entrance, KC saw a golf cart pull up and

leave the motor running.

Lo came back with an overflowing tray. "I'll meet you over there," he said, walking toward a newly-vacated booth.

"My ride just pulled up. I should go." Mayor Berger squeezed KC's hands. "I'm glad you're safe. We're proud of you. All of you." She made a hasty retreat to the exit.

KC sat down to eat with Lo, who had arranged their dishes on the table for maximum enjoyment. Through the window, she saw the Mayor of Kapualani Ranch hustle Mayor Berger into his golf cart. The Mayor drove them away before anyone else noticed.

"Why wouldn't she want to be seen?" KC asked.

"If they're at this hole in the wall, maybe they're having an affair," Lo said. "Is that why you brought me here?"

"I thought *you* brought *me*."

36. We're ready.
Mon night, Nov 03, 2014.

"They planned for this."

"They knew it was coming."

At the committee meeting, Miss Lani paged through KC's blueprints. "KC, these are perfect."

KC pumped her fist in the air at Lo, who was tickled by her enthusiasm.

"The island's population hasn't grown as much as the Founders' plans had projected at this point but, based on my research," Miss Lani took out her reports, "the infrastructure was already built in anticipation for a continuous net increase in residents."

"What are you saying with that fancy talk?" Scully asked, holding up a saucy meatball stuck to her fork.

"Our town already has most of what we need," KC explained. "All we have to do is open the buildings and get the systems up and running."

"And find the money to pay for it," Lo said.

"We pay taxes!" Hitchcock shouted.

Miss Lani absorbed the documents. "I'll ask Shira to come to next week's meeting and see how we can move forward."

Harlan gave his wife a thumbs-up. "Better be room in

there for my fountain."

...

After the meeting adjourned, KC and Lo exited the building and strolled in the direction of the San Marino cluster.

Once they were out of sight of the other committee members, KC held Lo's hand. "I had a nice time with you yesterday."

"When can we do it again?" Lo asked, as they ambled along the sidewalk.

"You're the one with the busy schedule."

"How about Thursday?"

"I'm going to a movie with the book club."

"Friday?"

"Swan has Friday night dinner."

"Could you invite a guest?"

"Probably, if I asked."

Lo stopped walking. "Does Swan know we're together?"

"We had our first official date yesterday. Do your friends know we're together?"

"No, but you've had dinner with my family. Why don't you want me to have dinner with yours?"

"I moved too fast last time. And the time before that." KC kept walking toward San Marino B. "I'm not ready yet. I need to set boundaries."

"I respect your boundaries. I will be here when you are

ready."

"I am available Saturday after I see my therapist."

"Does she know about us?"

KC stopped in front of the path to her front door. "I'm sure she'll know before I say a word."

37. If you say so.
Fri night, Nov 07, 2014.

"It's all vegetables!"

"But it tastes like chicken!"

"I know, right?"

At the dining table in Swan's apartment, KC devoured the protein chunks in her romaine salad. "I didn't believe it until I tried it at lunch on Wednesday."

"So good!" Shalom squealed.

"At least it's no rabbit," Swan said to her father.

"If there's ever a natural disaster," Poobah replied, "you'll be glad you have a survivalist in the family."

"We did have a natural disaster," Shalom said, refilling her glass of hibiscus tea.

"When?" Poobah asked.

Miguelito shook his body in his chair. "*Le tremblement de terre*, last month."

"Poobah," Shira said, "though it was unexpected, I liked the stew." She turned to KC. "And I like the salad."

"Thank you," Poobah and KC responded.

"Did it come from Bean's Greens?" Shira asked KC.

KC nodded, as she chewed her salad.

"A favorite of yours?" Swan queried of her girlfriend.

"I've only walked past the building," Shira said, "but Lo suggested I try their quinoa wrap. When I ran into him yesterday, he mentioned you liked the sundried tomatoes inside, KC."

KC stopped chewing.

Shalom stirred the tea. "Who's Lo?"

Shira remained silent, expecting KC to answer, but she said nothing.

"Doesn't he teach Kung Fu? Or Jiu-Jitsu?" Miguelito pondered.

"Karate," KC mumbled.

Swan noticed KC's shift in mood.

Shira availed herself of a biscuit. "I'm glad you two are on the committee. I hear you and Lo make a great team."

KC looked away.

"You and Lo?" Swan stated.

"It started this weekend," KC said.

Shira sliced the biscuit open. "Really? I thought it was earlier than..."

"Huh." Swan placed her metal utensils on her ceramic plate.

Shalom continued eating, unfazed, while Poobah and Miguelito got nervous.

"I'm taking it slow," KC uttered in Swan's direction.

168

"Okay," Swan acceded.

"I'm looking forward to seeing the committee's progress on Monday," Shira conveyed to KC.

"We're doing a bang-up job, if I do say so myself."

Swan picked up her fork and knife again.

KC scrutinized Swan's nonverbal communiqués. "We haven't even gone on a second date yet."

Swan concentrated on her full plate. "I see."

"Swan, if you have something to say, then say it!"

Swan returned her utensils to her napkin and rolled back from the table. She gave KC an open-arm shrug.

KC dug into her bed of greens like a petulant child, annoyed at Swan's lack of reaction.

Shalom didn't care.

Miguelito spun toward his ex-father-in-law. "So, Poobah, how's that embarrassing personal situation you didn't want to bring up at the dinner table?"

Poobah responded, "It's going terribly. Let's discuss it in detail and prevent anyone else from talking."

38. Five more points from Gryffindor.
Sat afternoon, Nov 08, 2014.

"Let's make room for the board."

"I found the letters."

"Holders. One for you, one for me."

In a cushioned booth at The Players' Club Bar & Grill on the Kapualani Ranch waterfront, KC set each of the brown plastic devices on the table between her and Lo.

Taking care not to disturb their appetizer wheel, Lo emptied the cardboard container to make sure everything came out.

"Seven tiles, right?" He opened the velour pouch and held it out for KC.

She grabbed a handful of letters and arranged them on her holder. "You can go first."

"You sure?"

"Go ahead," KC confirmed. She shook the plastic hourglass before putting it away.

Lo selected his tiles, and then reached into his pocket.

KC cleared the rest of the unnecessary items off the table, including a lined notepad, which she stowed in the Scrabble box. "We don't need to keep score."

Lo surreptitiously shoved the pad and pencil he had

been preparing back into his pocket.

While they dined on cheese curds, fried wontons, spinach and artichoke dip, and tortilla chips and tomatillo salsa, KC and Lo pored over their tile placements, trying to read each other's poker faces as they played the game.

"That's the last one." Lo crafted a three-letter word with his final pieces.

"Great job us." KC high-fived Lo over the loaded board.

A referee-styled waiter came by to clear their plates. "Thanks, Gavin," Lo said to him.

As he balanced his tray, Gavin read the array of simple words. "CAT. DOG. BIG. BIRD? You get rusty, brah?"

"We used all the letters," Lo replied, innocently.

Gavin wasn't buying it. "Is this the same spelling bee champion who knows all the words in eleventy languages? He always had double and triple word scores on his board back in the day."

"Oh, did he?" KC spied Gavin's amusement at Lo's discomfort.

Lo frowned and shook his head at Gavin, who shrugged and left with the tray of dishes. "This lolo."

"Are you taking it easy on me?" KC asked Lo.

"Are you?"

"Rematch."

KC and Lo played another, more competitive round of Scrabble, still with no official score, but the letter arrangements were more complex.

"Challenge!" Lo shouted.

"It's a word." KC searched for the mini dictionary in the box. "When I look it up, you're going to lose all your nonrecorded points."

Gavin floated by their booth. "I knew you two were a pair of Gryffindors pretending to be a Ravenclaw and a Hufflepuff."

KC and Lo pointed at each other. "You're Hufflepuff. You're Hufflepuff. You're Hufflepuff!"

...

KC and Lo stepped off the bus and walked to the door of KC's building.

Lo took KC's hands as they stood in front of the entrance.

"Why didn't you tell me you were good at Scrabble?" KC asked him

"I didn't want to look dorky."

"I'm the one who picked the game."

"I didn't know you were good at it." Lo wrung his hands. "And I had a bad experience before."

"Do you want to talk about it?"

"It was during my first year of university. Before I met Talon. I was hanging out in the common room of my dorm, horsing around with some other guys who lived down the hall. One of them opened a big drawer full of board games and pulled out Monopoly. He asked us if we wanted to play. Then he looked at me and said, 'You're good at this, right?' I think his name was Chad."

"Sounds like a Chad."

"I asked him why I'd be good at Monopoly. He told me, 'Asians are good at math. Like Jews are good at counting money.' Then he pulled out another box out of the drawer and asked my friend Hari if he'd rather play Scrabble, and said, 'Spelling bees, right?'"

"Ugh."

"Because Hari was Indian."

"I gathered."

"Still is. He's a firefighter in the Bronx."

"So what happened?"

"We played poker instead. Texas hold 'em."

KC waited for the rest of the story.

Lo was finished.

"That's it?"

"It wasn't a hate crime, but I wasn't used to people throwing stupid stereotypes at me. That wasn't a common occurrence where I grew up, meaning here. And I wished I had told him that India is a country in Asia too."

KC covered her face and rolled her eyes. She chose her words carefully. "Your feelings about those microaggressions are valid."

"Thank you."

"When I was in my first year of college, my roommate told me that I only got in because the school had a Spanish quota and that she didn't want any of my gangbanger baby daddies coming over to deal drugs out of our suite."

Lo blinked. His mouth remained shut.

KC squeezed his hands. "I like dorky."

Lo moved in closer. "How much do you like dorky?"

"A lot."

"A lot a lot?"

KC swung Lo's arms. "I will see you again when?"

"Whenever you like. Tomorrow. The next day. Right now. I am standing directly in front of you with no place to go for a couple hours."

KC stepped back. "Boundaries."

"Then I will be a vampire."

"I don't want a hickey."

"Not your neck. I won't enter your home until you invite me in."

"I'll be ready, eventually."

"There's no rush. Your health and wellness are important to me."

KC brought Lo's hand close to her face. She kissed his two fingertips. "I'll see you Monday night."

Lo brought his lips close to her ear. "I'll bring dessert."

39. Wait for it.
Mon night, Nov 10, 2014.

"What do you mean, 'circumstances have changed'?"

"Quiet down, please," Shira said to Scully and the rest of the committee members in Conference Room C.

The small gathering was in an uproar.

"Thank you, Shira," the Mayor said, standing at the head of the table. "As I was saying, the Mayors' Council is holding a special meeting this week."

Lo leaned in. "All the mayors?"

Shira responded, "All 25 of them." She looked at KC. "24 now."

Lo sat back in his chair to take in this information.

"Right here on the island," the Mayor continued, "to discuss the possible future of Kapualani Ranch. So, proposals for expansion for any town on Hale Kupua—"

"There are only two towns," Miss Lani said.

"—will be tabled until after the Council Meeting."

The committee remained incensed and yelled incoherently.

The Mayor shuffled toward the exit. "Great talk, people. I need to dash to another appointment."

"Where is he going?" Hitchcock wondered aloud.

Scully shrugged.

"You take it from here, Shira," the Mayor tossed.

The committee yelled at him with anger.

"Thank you, thank you," he said, as he fixed himself a plate with a pile of dessert on the way out.

The door shut behind him.

Lo sighed. "I made those brownies."

Miss Lani leaned back. "Shira, what is going on?"

Shira stood up. She placed her hands on the tabletop. "Kapualani Ranch is poised to become the next Reubenville—the center of government and business operations for Homestead. If the mayors vote to make Kapualani Ranch the next capital..."

"Then our whole discussion would be moot," KC finished.

"Why?" Lo asked.

"When you live in the capital," KC said, "you have access to anything you want. Within reason. And, at a price."

"But how would that affect 'Ohana Circle?" Lo probed. "Would this get us what we've been asking for?"

KC pushed away the plate in front of her. "And then some."

Lo stayed quiet for the rest of the meeting.

Miss Lani let out a deep exhale.

Shira looked concerned. "We'll have a better idea of how to move forward after the mayors convene, so I'll be back with you all next Monday, same time, same place. For now, let's see if our own mayor left us any brownies."

As the committee members dispersed, Lo move to retrieve his plastic brownie dish.

He found Scully wrapping and stuffing as many chocolate squares into her bag as possible. She yelled at Lo, "I'm eating for two!"

Lo tugged at the dish. "Two what?"

Scully used one hand to clutch her pearls. "How dare you!"

At the back the room away from the rest of the group, Shira waved KC over to converse with her and Miss Lani.

"What's your take on this?" Shira murmured to KC.

"It's a lot."

Shira took out a sheet of paper. "The mayors arrive tomorrow. Opening breakfast on Wednesday morning at the Singh Along Suites. Preliminary discussion at the legislature, followed by a press briefing at lunch, afternoon presentation, and the open public forum at 6:00 pm. Miss Lani can attend the forum, but KC, can you come to the afternoon block? I'll have a pass for you at the door."

KC shrugged. "Well, I'll have to ask my boss. Shira?"

"I'm not your boss. Who *is* your boss?"

"We still haven't figured that out. One of the reasons for this committee." KC glanced at the tug-of-war between Lo and Scully, with Hitchcock providing color commentary. "I'll be there."

...

After the meeting dispersed, KC and Lo paced tranquilly to the San Marino cluster.

"You've been quiet since the meeting," KC said. "Except for when you were fighting with a pregnant woman."

"I let her have the plate, didn't I? She better bring it back."

"What do you think about this island becoming the capital of Homestead?"

"It's complicated."

They arrived at KC's walkway.

KC waited for Lo to explain. He said nothing, so she poked his side.

"Ouch."

"How do you have no fat anywhere?"

"It's my stomach."

"Poke my stomach."

Lo pushed his finger on KC's side.

"See?"

Lo moved his finger around.

"That tickles! Stop distracting me. Tell me what you're thinking."

Lo dropped his hands to his sides. "I'm realizing I don't know what I don't know. I've traveled to all of the

Homestead communities with Pikake Beats and performed for every one of the mayors, but there are levels to the network I don't know if I can imagine."

"Same here. Not the performing part, but the levels. So many."

"But you know they exist. You have an informed opinion about this situation. I need to learn more before I make a willfully ignorant statement. No, I *will* learn more, before the next meeting."

KC lit up like a Roman candle. She pulled Lo into a quick, but intense kiss, which caught him by surprise.

"What was that for?" Lo asked, enchanted by KC's actions.

"You're doing the work." KC clapped to herself with satisfaction.

Lo shimmied his shoulders back and forth at KC. "You can get some of this work."

"Don't be gross."

40. Democracy in action.
Wed afternoon, Nov 12, 2014.

"I was standing there."

"You're in my way."

Along with a few other patrons, KC departed the bus and walked toward the City Hall entrance. She lowered her black Ray Bans from the crown of her ponytailed head to the bridge of her nose, which made room for her beige fedora. The hat matched KC's lightweight trench coat which, though unlined, was making her sweat through her floral blouse in the tropical fall weather.

"Excuse me." KC struggled to make her way through the agitated crowd up the steps to the carved double doors of the building. She attempted to follow the people who had gotten off the bus before, but they had stopped moving forward.

KC watched them jostle for places on the sidewalk in front of the building. Once settled in their personal locations, they removed various items from their satchels, including folded protest signs, professional grade cameras, and campaign t-shirts featuring the faces of Homestead politicians.

KC nudged her neighbors. "I'm trying to get through."

Occupied by their own business, no one listened.

KC stood stymied by the growing swarm surrounding City Hall. She peered around the corner for a sign to a back entrance.

Finally, the doors opened.

Shira stepped out onto the front stoop. She shielded her eyes from the sunlight. "KC?" she called into the teeming mass.

"That's me!" KC stuck her hand into the air. A pocket of space emerged before her. She dashed up the opening and up the stairs.

"I didn't think the protest would be this big and ornery already," Shira said to KC, once she had scaled the six feet of steps. "Considering it's not even 5:00 yet."

From the top of the staircase, KC had a clearer perspective of the gathering. She realized it was a chaotic mélange of factions with three separate motivations: protesting the event, photographing the news, and cheering for the celebrity mayors. But they were all mixed in together.

KC relayed her observation to Shira. "There aren't any designations for who goes where."

Shira regarded KC's ensemble. "And where do you go, Polynesian Carmen Sandiego?"

KC pulled her chapeau further down her forehead. "You know I'm not supposed to have any communication outside of my assigned community. I wanted to keep a low profile."

"Maybe if you were at a convention of cartoon spies."

Below the two women, the crowd swelled in size and sound.

"We have volunteers who should be roping off the area in a half hour," Shira said. "I certainly don't want to get the peacekeepers involved."

"We could do it ourselves."

"Us?"

"You are the Executive Director of the entire island."

"You're right," Shira said to KC. "Sometimes I forget." Shira waved her hands in the air above her head. "Hey!" she yelled over the din.

The crowd quieted down.

"Who has a press pass?" Shira asked.

A sprinkling of individuals held up the plastic rectangles hanging from the lanyards around their necks.

"Over here." Shira directed them to the area on her right.

They moseyed quietly.

"Who has a cardboard sign? Over there." Shira guided the protestors to her left. "Everyone else, stay put. Now you all have your own space."

KC looked at the newly-organized crowd. "That looks better."

"But I can't see." A voice called from the center of the camera people.

"Me either." Another voice echoed from the fans.

A taller protestor placed her placard on a step. "What about this?"

The news outlets, fans, and protestors politely debated amongst themselves who should stand where and adjusted themselves accordingly.

Shira put her hands on her hips. Her suggested

placement had provided the best impact for each group. However, the members of the crowd decide to arrange themselves by height, so that everyone could see, even though this mixed the protestors, fans, and photographers together.

"There!" The heterogeneous bunch, pleased with their arrangement, applauded their work.

Shira harrumphed.

"At least they're quiet," KC told Shira, who opened the heavy door for her.

Shira followed KC into the building, leaving a happier crowd. "You're just in time for the International Relations assessment."

As the two of them walked through the marble halls, KC reflected on how easily the crowd found harmony. "It's much harder to quell disorder outside of Homestead."

"That's why the network was created," Shira said. "It all began in Hale Kapua and spread across the world, one community at a time. Now the leadership is back where it started."

KC stopped in her tracks. "The Capital is coming here?"

"It's a possibility." Shira realized KC wasn't walking with her anymore. "That's what all of this is about, remember?"

KC's voice caught in her throat. "I remember."

41. I'm sorry.
Wed afternoon, Nov 12, 2014.

"Any questions?"

From the cloak of darkness on a bamboo bench in the back of the Great Room of City Hall, KC observed Alvester conclude his complex presentation to the panel of 24 visiting mayors, who were positioned in the front row. Each mayor's seat was distinguished by the country flag that represented their respective communities. She noticed Mayor Berger seated in an elevated chair in the row directly behind them, sans flag, next to Shira.

KC watched Alvester, garbed in one of his chocolate brown bespoke suits, as he stood on stage in front of the final, intricate slide projected onto the bright screen, waiting for a response to his inquiry of the panel.

After an extended shuffling of weary bottoms in seats, the center representative rose to her feet.

"Yes, Mayor Barnaby-Jacks?" Alvester acknowledged.

"Thank you, Mr. Kao," the mayor said. "This is a lot to take in."

The other overwhelmed mayors murmured in agreement.

Mayor Barnaby-Jacks addressed her peers. "I move that we take a brief recess to digest your demonstration of the chaos theory that could result as a consequence of our proposal. Let's regroup in 15 minutes."

The other mayors concurred with a unanimous "Aye," then exited their seats, and milled about the venue.

After departing the stage, Alvester surprised KC by walking past the score of elected officials dispersed throughout the grand room, down the carpeted center aisle, directly toward her.

"Hey."

"Hey." KC bristled. She stood up next to Alvester.

"It's kinda crazy, huh?"

"You did a good job."

"I did my best. What do you think of this hullabaloo?"

KC looked at mayors' vacated, decorated seats. "I have visited every one of those communities, and I have shaken every one of those mayors' hands. Yet I still couldn't tell you which flag is which."

Alvester laughed. "I know what you mean. US and Canada, no problem. Japan has a big dot. Mexico and France, red stripe. But then you have countries with the variations on either the stars and stripes or the Union Jack, and you've lost me."

KC relaxed. "It's easier when everyone is sitting down."

"Yeah."

They each took a deep breath, less tense than before.

"I'm sorry," KC blurted out. "I know I said it then, but I'm sorry. I wasn't in a good place, and it wasn't fair to put you in that position. I'm getting better. It doesn't excuse what I did."

Some of the mayors looked in her direction.

KC realized her voice was bouncing off the walls. She motioned for Alvester to follow her into the hallway.

Once they were outside the room, Alvester touched her arm. "I accept your apology."

"I didn't know what to say after you had my suitcase delivered with that note. I didn't know what to say at the Halloween party. Your date seemed nice."

"Rhoda? She is nice. She liked you."

"Did she say that?"

"She said you didn't seem as crazy as rumored."

"I'll take it." KC noticed additional people walking through the halls. Shira and her volunteer team were strategizing for the public forum that was next on the agenda for the afternoon. Mayor Barnaby-Jacks was engaged in an intimate conversation with a dark-haired gentleman wearing wrinkled chinos. The Mayor of Kapualani Ranch was consuming a ham sandwich.

Alvester unbuttoned his suit jacket. "I don't know if you caught all of it, but that was a grueling session in there. For me, anyway. And for you, yes? The consideration of Kapualani Ranch as the new capital must be triggering."

"Yes! It is," KC confirmed, shaking her palms at Alvester. She heard Mayor Barnaby-Jacks let out a peal of laughter at her companion's joke. "Will no one else think of the refugees? I was trying to put my thoughts into those words the other night, when I was walking home with Lo."

Alvester flinched. "Right."

KC blanched. "We're—"

"I heard."

"It's new."

"It's alright. He's a good guy."

"You're a good—" KC was sidetracked by a guffaw coming from a familiar face in her eyeline. She recognized the man bantering with Mayor Barnaby-Jacks. "Lo?"

42. No taxation without representation.
Wed night, Nov 12, 2014.

"KC?" In the same hallway, Lo turned away from Mayor Barnaby-Jacks to spot KC standing next to Alvester.

KC, followed by Alvester, walked across the marble tiles to the other pair.

Lo, flustered, introduced the people in front of him. "Mia, this is KC. KC, this is Mayor Mia Barnaby-Jacks, Head of the Mayors' Council. She's from Lake Elmo, the Homestead community in the Northern Territory in Australia."

"We've met," KC told Lo.

Behind the tense quartet, Shira and her team started letting a torrent of attendees into the Great Room, directing them to their seats in a speedy, yet orderly fashion.

"KC, it's good to see you again." Mia gave her a hug. "I'm glad to see you got out okay. How have you been?"

"Better every day," KC replied. "Do you know Alvester?"

"Of course," Lo said. He pulled him in for an awkward hug. "Howzit, brother?"

Alvester hugged back and added some fist bumps. "Good good, brother."

KC furrowed her brow at the men's exchange. "I meant

Mia. Well, obviously from in the room a few minutes ago."

Alvester slipped away from Lo's grasp to shake Mia's hand. "We've crossed paths many times."

"And every time it's a pleasure." Mia rotated the pearl and diamond-encrusted wedding band around her finger. "I should go rally the troops before the forum starts. The Council sounds like it's getting restless." Mia gave KC another hug. "We miss you. All of you."

The four of them said their goodbyes, and Alvester and Mia reentered the Great Room, where a lively crowd had gathered inside, filling almost every seat. From outside the open door, KC witnessed Mia herd the other mayors back to the front row, while Alvester returned to the stage to retrieve his materials.

Lo rocked on his heels next to KC. "Are you going back in or heading out?"

"What would you prefer?" KC asked. "I wouldn't want to cramp your style."

Lo held out his hand.

KC took it.

They made their way inside the clustered room. KC found her previous space in the back. She and Lo rested on her bamboo bench.

Once the mayors settled back into position, Mayor Barnaby-Jacks took the stage. She welcomed the audience to the afternoon's event and opened the floor for questions. "We have microphones on either side, and I see you've already started to form queues, so we'll start on my right."

KC watched the residents of Hale Kupua demand difficult answers from the Mayors' Council about their proposal, inquiring about topics ranging from political tourism to transportation infrastructure to environmental impact.

Meanwhile, Lo fidgeted on the hard wood.

"What's wrong?" KC whispered.

Lo shook his head. "I'll tell you later." He looked straight ahead at the mayor from Panama, who was responding to a question about banana-trade expectations.

KC looked straight at Lo. "Tell me now."

"I slept with Mia."

43. Differing opinions.
Wed night, Nov 12, 2014.

"You slept with Mia? In the biblical sense?"

With the steady cacophony generated between the mayors and the general audience in the Great Room in the Kapualani Ranch City Hall, no one else heard KC's astonished cry.

"Outside," Lo motioned.

KC and Lo squeezed past their fellow citizens into the hallway and out the side doors of the building onto the sidewalk, before continuing their conversation.

As the sun set in the distance, coloring the sky a shade of magenta that contrasted with the cobalt blue of the harbor, the two of them found a space away from the governmental commotion.

KC waited for an explanation.

Lo huffed. "It was years ago."

"Years ago? Was that even legal?"

"Five years ago. So..." Lo counted in his head. "Yes. It was in Lake Elmo during one of the first Pikake Beats tours. Before she was married. What are you doing?"

"Processing." KC marched back and forth along the rock garden bordering City Hall.

"Did you have a nice talk with Alvester?"

KC didn't break stride. "We spoke for maybe five minutes," she said, on her third lap.

Lo joined her loop, following step by step.

"Is this funny to you?" KC asked her new shadow.

"What do you want to know?"

KC came to an abrupt halt, causing Lo to bump tummy first into her trench coat. "Are you still interested in her?"

"It was a one-time thing."

"So you weren't very good."

"I was excellent!" Lo insisted. "But she was doing her campaign thing, and I was doing my performance thing. We were two ships passing in the night on different roads on the wings of our dreams. It didn't make sense."

"Neither did that metaphor."

"What about Alvester?" Lo rebutted.

"I liked his presentation."

Lo waited.

KC took a moment to cogitate. She looked up at Lo. "I am only interested in you."

"I am only interested in you."

"Good."

"Okay then."

KC grasped for both of his strong hands. "Did you get to see any of the events today?"

"At City Hall? I had just arrived when you saw me. But I have been reading up on this Capital business in the Homestead papers online."

"And?" KC smiled in anticipation.

Lo admitted, "I'm not sure what to think yet."

KC glowered.

"But I'm glad the people of Hale Kupua are being heard," Lo declared with pride.

KC kept her fingers intertwined with his, but she crooked her head away to grunt her exasperation.

Lo leaned in for a better listen. "What was that?"

"Nothing."

44. I know stuff.
Fri night, Nov 14, 2014.

"Then she said, 'I've never been to Minnesota!'"

Balancing her mixed berry pie in one hand, KC concentrated on opening the door to Swan's apartment with her other. She backed into the clamor of laughter emanating from the group in the living room after the delivery of the punch line.

"You're here!" Shalom helped KC inside. "I'll put this on the counter."

"Lo, you are too funny!"

In the entryway, KC swiveled to find Shira chuckling in the easy chair along Poobah and Miguelito sitting on the couch, cackling at the person who was sandwiched between them.

Miguelito agreed with Poobah's assessment. *"Comme c'est drôle!"*

"Surprise!" Swan rolled out of the kitchen toward KC with her hands up.

"What's going on?" KC peered at Lo, who was standing up to greet her.

"Swan invited me to Friday night dinner." Lo gave KC a hug, while KC left her arms pressed against her sides.

"I see." KC maneuvered her mouth into the smile the others were expecting. "Genial."

"Are we ready to eat?" Poobah moved from the living room to the dining table, which KC noticed had a leaf wedged in the center of it, along with an extra chair nestled next to KC's regular spot.

"Unless there are any other guests?" Shira followed Poobah to the table.

KC held the door open. "Swan?"

"You're the last one," Swan replied.

"Somehow I beat you here tonight." Shira sat down at her place.

Miguelito and Shalom joined Shira, and Swan showed Lo where to sit.

KC shut the door and had a seat. "Seems like tonight's full of surprises."

...

"No verdict yet," Shira told Poobah, as they dined on the potluck meal. "The Mayors' Council will meet again in Lake Elmo next month to debate more viewpoints. But the committee sessions will continue, even though the capital decision is in limbo."

"That sucks." Shalom checked her phone while she slurped her tea.

"Coincidentally," Lo interjected, "I will also be in Lake Elmo next month."

Swan noticed that KC was eyeing Lo like a zoo exhibit.

"The Pikake Beats Holiday tour?" Shira asked. "It's an amazing show, even bigger than what you all saw at the Welcome Luau."

Lo nodded and swallowed. "Starts in two weeks. We leave the day after Thanksgiving; back the day before Christmas Eve. The twins are staying with my parents, but

Snow Belle's performing on the summer tour when we take out the kids' troupe. First stop this season is Arco Iris. Isn't that where your friend's from?" Lo asked KC.

"Which friend?" KC stiffened.

"The one we saw at Kau Kau. Her name's Berger?" Lo offered.

Shalom stopped shoveling food into her mouth. "You saw Mayor Berger? She's the best."

"She's not from Arco Iris," KC corrected. "She lives there now after we were ousted from our home."

A gloomy cloud fell over the table.

Shalom kept eating and texting, unperturbed.

Swan smiled at Lo. "Mayor Berger is the best."

After one final bite, Shalom took her emptied plate to the kitchen sink. "Hollis and Brooklyn are hanging out at the Monkey Bar."

"Great smoothies," Lo offered.

"That's true," KC confirmed.

Lo beamed at the acknowledgement.

Shalom typed on her phone. "Can I go? I finished my dinner."

"What about dessert?" Swan asked her daughter.

Shalom retrieved a plastic box from the cabinet, scooped up a serving of pie inside, and stuffed the box in her jacket. "I'll eat it on the bus."

"Fine. See you later," Swan said.

As Shalom was hugging her mother on the way out, Miguelito voiced, "Isn't anyone going to ask me about this?"

Shalom paused mid-hug.

Swan shared her daughter's confusion but allowed the question. "What are your thoughts?"

Miguelito handed Shalom a napkin. "The tarte with the berries is messy. Also, *un bisou*, please."

Shalom kissed her father's cheek. "Bye, Dad."

"Lo brought the Spam musubi," Shira informed KC, as Shalom walked out the door.

KC placed her fork down. "That's not vegan."

"It's barely meat," Poobah said.

"That's your third helping," Miguelito said to him.

"And this is my fourth." Poobah scooped another saucy, seaweed-wrapped block of rice onto his plate.

Lo placed his palm on KC's upper arm. "I brought it because I thought you would like it."

"Oh. Thank you."

"How does it taste?" Lo asked her.

"Surprising."

Lo took his hand back.

...

"Thank you for having me." Lo hugged Swan goodbye after the adults had finished their dessert.

"I will see you at the pick up game on Sunday?" Miguelito confirmed with Lo.

"You know it, brah." Lo clapped him on the back. "And Poobah, we've got Tai Chi at the Downtown center until we open up on the East End."

"I have signed up, and my sweatpants are ready," Poobah replied.

"See you Monday night," Lo said to Shira.

Shira gave him a hug. "I'm glad you were here."

KC nudged Lo toward the hall. "I'll walk you out."

When the two of them reached front door of the building, Lo lingered in the placid vestibule.

"I survived," he said to himself.

"A meal that wasn't entirely vegetables?" KC queried.

"Your family," Lo clarified. "They're intimidating."

"You're intimidated? By them?"

"You're so used to the circles you run in, you don't even notice," Lo said. "I'm sitting at a table with three government officials, two famous footballers, and one new girlfriend. And one Poobah."

"Fortunately for you, they're all the same people. And they all like you. And you're a celebrity yourself."

"Yeah, right."

"Am I the one headlining a five-continent tour at the end of the month with the dance troupe I founded?"

"No, that's me," Lo recalled.

"Am I the one that brought Spam rolls to dinner to impress their 'new girlfriend'?" KC air quoted.

"Me again. Did it work?"

KC wrapped her arms around Lo's neck. "Yeah."

Lo inched closer. "Yeah?"

She pressed her forehead against his. "Yeah."

Lo discerned the vulnerability in KC's face give way to comfort. He proceeded with caution as he kissed her tenderly.

KC returned the kiss with a passion that crackled from her heated earlobes to her curled toes.

It excited Lo.

But it scared KC.

She pulled away.

Lo retreated, searching for a sign of how to respond.

KC opened the door for him. "Thanks for coming to dinner."

"Thanks for letting me come."

KC smirked.

"Come to dinner?" Lo said. "Are you 12?"

"Goodnight."

After Lo left the building, KC held the door open with her body, watching him walk away.

Then she shut the door.

45. Roses and chocolate.
Sun morning, Nov 16, 2014.

"Chocolate?"

"No, this is my skin."

Outside the entrance of the 'Ono Market, KC offered Swan a dark fleur de sel caramel from the candy box she was referring to. "So you're the funny one now?"

"You're rubbing off on me." Swan selected a piece. *"Pas mal."* She ate another one. "Are they from here?"

KC pushed her manual cart next to Swan's motorized version. "Lo had a gift basket with white roses delivered to my apartment earlier. Along with this." She handed Swan a typed card with a yellow daisy on the front.

"'I'm sorry for whatever I did.' What did he do?"

"He didn't do anything wrong," KC said. "But I felt some kind of way."

"About what?"

KC was thinking.

Swan was waiting.

"Do you remember the New Year's Eve pre-party I threw at my building in Reubenville last year?" KC asked. "I changed it from a dance contest to a sit-down dinner because Morrow told me that Noa was pregnant and grumpy?"

"And because we weren't in junior high school," Swan added.

"Anyways," KC pushed a carton of macarons into her cart, "for some reason, I couldn't stop thinking about that Friday night dinner, even though they were completely different."

"Six or seven people, instead of twelve."

KC counted, "It was me, you, Shira—"

"Kimber, Dr. Tom, and those two friends of yours from Lake Elmo?"

"Sasha and Antonio, yes, they were on vacation. Shalom wasn't there?"

"No, she was babysitting so Mariska and Declan could come."

"Declan." KC stopped. "I'm still mad at him for all this."

"It would have happened regardless." Swan rolled forward.

"He didn't have to help it along."

"He told me he didn't think he had a choice. Provide information, or Red Spore would threaten his family."

"I hope they're safe."

"Kimber made sure of it. Wherever they are."

KC kept moving. "And Topher."

Swan perused the shelves.

KC searched for the best words. "It felt..."

"Familiar?"

"Yes, but... Maybe because you and Shira were both there."

"That makes sense."

"And familial," KC said. "Uncomfortably so."

"You were happy at the New Year's Eve party. What was different on Friday?"

"I wasn't ready!" KC balled her hands into fists. "I didn't know Lo would be there."

"That's why it's called a surprise," Swan said. "I was trying to show you that I support your decisions."

"I'm having too many feelings at once."

Swan directed KC and their carts into a calmer corner of the store. "I liked having Lo at dinner. Why didn't you?"

"Why didn't you invite Alvester to dinner before? You like him more than Lo."

"Yes, I would have preferred if you had stayed with Alvester. But I'm not the one dating him. And Lo has his unrefined charms. He's definitely an upgrade from... previous partners." Swan looked away.

"You didn't like Topher?"

"I did at first," Swan confessed.

"Why didn't you say something?"

"Like what?"

"'Your boyfriend's a scumbag'?"

"Would you have listened?"

"No."

"Also, I didn't know immediately. I had to learn, like you did. But there were signs."

"What signs?"

Swan groaned. "He was too pretty."

"He couldn't control that."

"But he was not humble." Swan gathered her words. "As if he knew his power had an expiration date, so he wielded it as recklessly as possible. I don't know Lo that well, but he recognizes that with his own great power comes great responsibility. I trust him. Again, I'm not the one dating him."

"I need to go." KC walked toward the front entrance of the market.

"What about your groceries?" Swan called to her from the back corner.

"It's a box of cookies." KC pointed to the lone item in her abandoned cart. "I'll buy another one next Sunday."

After stopping at each sample booth to try the foods on display—"Everything here tastes so good."—KC barreled outside, sidestepping the customers in the checkout aisles.

KC pressed the video chat feature on her phone.

"Hello!" Lo beamed from KC's screen, the lagoon waves crashing behind him.

"The basket is wonderful." KC continued walking south through the streets of 'Ohana Circle. "I don't know why I was mad on Friday. I do know that it wasn't your fault."

"So you liked the basket?"

"I love you, I mean, *it*. I love it. Thank you. The basket. Why are you smiling?"

Lo snorted, seawater dripping from his hair onto his nose. "I love the basket too. So why were you mad?"

"I was surprised. Confused. I'm fine."

"Your phone keeps moving. Where are you going?"

KC came to an intersection. She looked behind her at the housing clusters on the hill. Then she looked at the horizon in front of her. "Are you surfing today?"

"It's Sunday, so yes. I'll be at Big Beach till lunchtime. And then I'll probably eat my poke here too. Unless you want to meet somewhere."

KC kept walking. "Stay there. I'll meet you where you are."

46. Georgia, Georgia.
Sun night, Nov 16, 2014.

As the orange sun sank into the haze of the blue lagoon, KC released Lo's hand.

Lo stayed on the sidewalk bordering the San Marino cluster. He was reluctant to leave, but he let her go.

KC padded backward up the pathway to the door of her building so that she could watch Lo walk away. Her nose was still streaked with a white coat of sunscreen, but her cheeks were lightly toasted.

KC took the elevator up to her apartment, with sand in-between her toes, feeling blissful.

Once inside, KC saw her laptop sitting on the coffee table. Her mood shifted from elation to apprehension.

She sat down and opened her computer. Then she clicked on the video in the center of the screen. Pachelbel's Canon in D hummed from the speakers.

KC skipped forward past the wedding ceremony and stopped at the reception, right after the camera captured the newlyweds cutting into a tiered cake surrounded by frosted cupcakes.

Two people danced into view of the camera, separated from the crowd of other celebratory guests.

"Is it our turn?"

KC saw a posher version of herself on the screen,

wearing a midnight blue-chiffon gown, her cheekbones and lips contoured, her hair flat-ironed. She was a stark contrast to the KC on the couch, in cutoff capri overalls, with a make-up free face and seawater mist clinging to her unbrushed curls.

"We're up."

A dapper man with light blue-green eyes and manicured stubble in a charcoal suit stood next to KC in the video.

"1, 2, 3!"

"Congratulations, Noa and Morrow!"

"Then we cheers with the cupcakes?"

"Nom, nom, nom."

"Topher! You got icing on my dress."

"There. Now I have icing on my jacket. We match."

"We fit together. Maybe forever?"

"Together forever? That's a long time."

"Are you scared that could be us?"

"Engaged and married in less than a month?"

"When you know, you know, KC."

"Do you know?"

"I think I do. Do you know?"

"I think I do. We, us?"

"Us. We. Wouldn't it be nice?"

"Could be, To."

"Let's go have our own wedding night."

"Are you still filming us?"

On the couch, KC watched the enamored twosome sprint out of sight before the video cut to additional well wishes from other congratulatory guests.

KC closed the laptop. Then she closed her eyes.

After a moment, she ended her meditation and strode to her hall closet.

KC pushed through a bundle of unused cleaning supplies to find an upright rolling suitcase hiding against the back wall. She opened the bag and pulled out the single item still left inside: a midnight-blue dress stained with cupcake icing.

Pinching each of the sleeves, KC held the garment out in front of her. She scrutinized the folds of the fabric, as if she could find an answer to her unasked question.

Unfulfilled, KC balled up the gown and prepared to toss it in the kitchen trash.

But she couldn't.

She wasn't ready.

KC carefully folded the dress, zipped it back into the full suitcase, and shoved the bag back in the hall closet.

She kicked the door shut with her sandy foot.

47. Say what?
Thu morning, Nov 27, 2014.

"No."

"No?"

"Nooo…"

"Well…"

"No!"

KC leaned her elbows on Swan's kitchen counter, scrolling through the *Current Messenger* news site her phone. "What even is this?"

Shira arranged the green bean casserole, yams, mashed potatoes, and kimchi on the counter to make room for the fancy plates and flatware. "Maybe there's more explanation at the end of the article?"

"I read his letter to the editor from top to bottom," KC said. "Twice. 'As a native Hale Kupuan, I want to share my perspective on the issues.'"

"Well, he started off strong," Swan said, relaxing in the dining area.

KC continued reading from the palm-sized screen. "'Lake Elmo has room, renown, and resources, as the entertainment capital of Homestead.' Why couldn't he end the letter there?"

"You're cooking more food?" Swan asked Shira, who

had opened the oven door.

"I'm checking on the turkey," Shira replied, as she slid a cookie tray on the rack under the bird.

"Then what are those?" Swan prodded.

"We need biscuits."

"We already have jalapeño cornbread, blueberry muffins, and dinner rolls."

"That's a lot of carbohydrates for the five of you," KC said.

"You're not staying?" Shira asked.

"She's going to Lo's parents' farmhouse," Swan reminded.

"That was the plan before this letter," KC said.

Shira closed the oven with the rising biscuit dough inside. "I'm sure Shalom, Miguelito, and Poobah will be extra hungry after they come home from the Turkey Bowl All Star game."

"They're watching the match, they're not playing football with the Junior Leaguers themselves," Swan countered.

"'But Kapualani Ranch upholds tradition as the founding community of Homestead,'" KC kept reading.

"Why don't you talk with Lo about this?" Swan asked KC. Then she shifted to Shira. "And why are you so into Thanksgiving?"

Shira removed her quilted mitts. "I relish the irony of celebrating colonization on an island established to escape the patriarchy."

"'Therefore I call for a referendum. An up or down vote'?" KC read, appalled. "'The people of the Homestead network should decide where the capital should move.'"

"That is not an informed opinion," Swan said.

"Up or down vote?!" KC screeched.

"Lo means well," Shira told KC. "He's an overachiever, like you two. But he doesn't have all the information."

KC set her phone next to the can of cranberry sauce. "As a native Californian, I can attest that when the people vote on every issue, it doesn't always turn out well."

Swan picked up KC's phone to finish the letter. "'In conclusion, Homestead is of the people, for the people, by the people. The people should be heard.'"

"Not all of them," KC muttered.

"Take one of these containers with you to the farmhouse," Swan told KC, handing her the phone. "Any one of them. And stop being mad at Lo for what he doesn't know. Tell him what you're afraid of."

KC folded her arms. "But he doesn't have the security clearance to understand anyway."

Shira surveyed the kitchen surfaces, still laden with enough items to feed an American football team. "Should I have attempted traditional Nigerian dishes as well?" she asked Swan.

"No."

KC complied. She placed the plastic tub of muffins into a reusable shopping bag, which she slung over her shoulder. "I will talk to him. I'm the people who should be heard."

48. Point break.
Thu afternoon, Nov 27, 2014.

"She's here!"

"Don't scare her, Mom."

In the Echo division of the Xochitl agricultural cluster, KC climbed up the steps of the covered front porch to the Welcome mat of Lo's parents' farmhouse.

Ms. Hobbs swooped her inside the open door with a hug. "Come in."

"The muffins are from Shira," KC said, showing the contents of her bag. "I made the fruit salad. Berry salad. I washed blackberries, raspberries, strawberries, and put them in a recyclable container. No animal products involved."

Mr. Gambon met them in the foyer. "Your salad is lovely, KC." He and his wife took KC's food to the kitchen.

KC heard a commotion coming from the living room, where the furniture had been pushed up against the wall for maximum floor space to accommodate the throng of bopping guests. "Where are Nala and Snow Belle?"

"Playing in the backyard with the other kids." Lo pulled KC into the dance party. "You're just in time. Everybody," Lo announced to the crowd. "This is KC." Lo gazed at KC with adoration.

From the kitchen, Lo's parents hugged each other, elated by their son's happiness.

In the living room, one family member paused mid-shoulder shimmy to whisper to her neighbor, "Is the curse over?"

Another family member replied, but kept her shimmy going. "We'll see."

Vin walked over. "Join the fun."

KC glanced at the eight counts that the other guests were practicing, a fusion of ballroom steps and interpretive arm movements. "I'm supposed to learn this Lambada waltz?"

"It's easy, no lie," Vin assured. "And it's called the *Salsa Fresca de la Playa*."

"It's new for all of us," Lo said. "We're going to debut in on the tour."

"So, tomorrow?" KC said. "It's easy for you," she told Vin. "You're all professional dancers."

"Not all of us," Lo denied.

KC shouted to the room, "Who in here dances for a living?"

The room was filled with raised hands. Even the dog lifted her paw.

Lo shook his head. "Not now, Mittens."

Mittens let out a sigh and lowered her paw.

Vin poked KC. "You practice. I'll get the song started."

"I'll show you how." Lo placed his hand on KC's side to guide her.

As KC enjoyed the warmth of his palm through her thin

sweater, the rest of the world fell away.

Lo stood to the left of KC. His body moved, and KC's body followed, to the best of her ability.

"It's a hula."

"I can't move my hips like yours," KC complained. "I wasn't born on a Pacific beach like you."

"I was born in a hospital, and yes, you can." Lo slid behind her.

KC blushed as Lo held her waist, the front of his pants grazing her back pockets. "To the right, to the right," Lo instructed, pressing KC's hip in the direction of his shuffle. "Then to the left, to the left. Now, box step with a cha cha."

KC matched Lo's feet and attempted the corresponding arm movements as well. "I'm getting it!"

"Great, now we're going to try it together."

"You and me at the same time?" KC whined.

"And everyone else. It's a group dance in pairs," Lo explained, as Vin found the music.

"I thought it was a line dance like the Electric Slide," KC said, watching the rest of the guests take their places. "I was going to stand in the back and pretend I know what I'm doing. But I don't."

Lo interlocked his fingers with KC's. He walked her to the center of the floor. " I do."

"I'll mess you up."

"I don't care."

Vin stood by the sound system. "Ready?"

"Are you?" Lo asked KC.

"Yes," she replied.

Lo nodded at Vin, who pressed play.

"Follow me," Lo told KC, as the music started.

"I'm not good at letting someone else lead."

"I'm shocked," Lo teased. "But you're doing fine."

KC observed the spins and flairs that the other dancers had added to their choreography. "How come we're not doing that?" She lifted her chin at one of Lo's cousins who executed a triple pirouette into a body roll and split.

Lo backed up to give KC room. "Go ahead."

KC pulled him back to her. "Never mind."

The two of them continued moving back and forth, side to side, up and down, absorbing each other's rhythms.

Lo nuzzled his nose into KC's neck. "I should take you on tour with me."

KC breathed in his ear. "You couldn't afford me."

...

"You're so sweaty."

"Thanks a lot!"

Sandwiched onto a wicker loveseat, Lo dabbed KC's glowing face with a cornucopia-themed paper napkin. "It just means we need to do this more often to increase your stamina. Still wish you could come with. But I will call you every day until I come back home."

Appropriately squeegeed, KC continued eating from her hubcap-sized plate, which held a sample of every dish brought by each of the three-dozen guests inside the farmhouse.

She looked around at the long tables filled with bowl after bowl of food and the smiling people occupying every available seat. "This looks a lot like Thanksgiving with my family."

Lo touched her knee. "Yeah?"

KC nodded, sadly.

"'Homestead is of the people, for the people, by the people.'" Vin read from Ms. Hobbs's electronic tablet.

"Doesn't it sound dignified?" Ms. Hobbs asked Vin, with pride.

KC released her fork.

"Presidential even," Vin smarmed at Lo. "Lincoln would be proud."

Ms. Hobbs brought her tablet over to KC. "Have you seen his letter?"

"Mom, she doesn't want to read that, she's eating."

The rest of the food remained untouched on KC's plate. "Yes, I have."

"You have?" Lo asked. "Why didn't you say anything?"

"Sonia!" Ms. Hobbs moved on to the next guest. "Look what Lo wrote."

KC found a side table to set down the rest of her meal. "I had forgotten about it with all the—" she gesticulated with her arms and torso.

"All the seizures?" Lo offered.

KC didn't laugh.

"You didn't like it." Lo surmised.

"Maybe I didn't understand your position."

"I think everyone should be heard. There are benefits to having the capital come here—"

KC searched for her phone.

"—but the decision shouldn't be made," Lo continued, "solely by our elected officials. It's simple."

"Simple." KC typed on her screen. "Then I did understand."

Lo, confounded by her response, stood up. "I'm going to get some mango pie, and then we can talk some more."

KC grabbed her bag. "Can we talk outside?"

KC led him to the front porch.

"I thought we were having fun," Lo said. "What happened?"

KC fought back tears. She refused to let her voice shake as she blurted out, "I need space. I need a break."

Lo's eyes widened.

"I'm sor—" KC watched as a taxi turned onto the driveway of the Xochitl cluster. "That's me."

Lo opened his mouth to speak, but uttered only, "I don't under—", then remained silent.

Vin came out of the house, bearing a paper plate stuffed with desserts. "KC, where are you going?"

Lo stood motionless.

KC walked to the car. "Have a good tour. Stay safe."

49. You're welcome.
Fri night, Nov 28, 2014.

"More stuffing please."

"Any more and you'll burst."

At Swan's dining table, KC replied to her friend, "I didn't get to finish my meal at the party yesterday."

Poobah chimed in, plopping a scoop on his plate before passing the bowl to KC, "I did, and I'm back for more."

Shalom swallowed her last bite and delivered her entire place setting to the kitchen sink.

"I'm glad you like it," Shira said to KC.

Miguelito consumed his own serving as well. "It tastes even better the next day."

Swan called to Shalom, who was reading *The Fantasy of My Reality* on the couch in her pajamas. "Is that all you're having?"

"I had a big lunch."

Swan turned to KC. "How was dinner last night?"

"Superb," KC said. "Until I broke up with Lo. You're welcome."

"How is this my fault?" Swan asked. "I told you to talk with him."

"I did."

"And what did he say?"

"Nothing new. So I ended it."

"*Encore une fois*," Miguelito inserted. "*Quelle surprise.*"

"Not now, Miguel," Swan scolded.

"Are you okay?" Shira asked KC.

The table waited.

KC answered with candor, "I'm not."

"How can we help?" Shira inquired.

"I felt safe here. Now I don't. It could happen again. Will it?"

Shira couldn't give KC an answer.

"What he doesn't know could hurt me... Us. Am I the only one who is scared?" KC lowered her chin, her eyes cast on the crumpled napkin on her lap.

Poobah sipped his tea. He set the cup on his saucer. "Whatever will be, will be."

"Yes, but," Swan trod lightly in response to her father's words, "waiting for the inevitable won't help KC feel better."

"Neither will denying the changes occurring in front of her," Miguelito injected.

"There's no change happening yet," Shira said.

"Yet," Miguelito emphasized, looking at Swan. "I wouldn't want her to be blindsided by a decision that someone had already made."

"It wasn't a choice," Swan said to him. "It was a realization."

"*Mais, mon couer*. My heart. *C'était cassé*."

Swan looked away, crestfallen.

"I'm scared." Shalom suddenly materialized at the table, startling KC. "So are my friends. Sometimes we talk about it. Our parents don't."

Poobah, Miguelito, and Swan all remained forlorn.

"We take care of each other," Shalom continued nonchalantly. "We feel our feelings. It's okay to feel yours," she affirmed for KC.

Directly across the table, Shira chose her words for KC with care. "The war is not over. Red Spore only won the first battle. But you will not be a casualty."

Miguelito and Poobah shared a puzzled expression.

Swan held Shira's hand.

KC appeared less morose.

"Now that we're sufficiently bummed out," Shalom said, "who wants to watch Black Friday stampedes."

KC refilled her dish, followed Shalom to the living room, and joined her on the couch to view the carnage.

50. Space and time.
Sat afternoon, Nov 29, 2014.

"Am I dumb? Am I an overeducated idiot?"

On the other side of her office, KC's therapist replied to her question with quizzical silence.

"Before Homestead," KC continued, "I never would have imagined I would live in the desert of Eastern California. There is nothing there. But some residents didn't want to leave. Reubenville was their land, the only home they had ever known. If we'd had more information, the Associates could have tried to prevent the invasion. I know Swan tells me it wasn't our fault, and Shira insists that the wrongs will be righted, but I blame myself.

"And since the evacuation effectively ended his assignment, Topher went home. Well, to DC. The DMV. Somewhere near the capital of the United States. Wherever he went, he didn't ask me to go with him."

KC slouched on the couch.

"If it happened here, where would I go next? Another Homestead community, obviously. I'm done with the outside. It can be a nice place to visit, if I'm seeing my family. But I can't live there. The network has spoiled me. My quality of life standards have grown too high, and my threshold for discriminatory nonsense is too low.

"There is a level of respect that I command in Homestead, which I am surprised has continued without being an Associate. Lo has the love of his family, and the island. He isn't viewed in the same way, but he is cherished."

KC slumped further down. "Lo is unable to comprehend

the situation. He's a naïve boy, and I'm a worldly girl. How am I battling white privilege on an island that has zero white people?!"

KC collapsed onto the couch cushions, exasperated.

"Isn't that the whole point of the Homestead network, living in our own world without the jackboots of the patriarchy planted on our necks? I guess wherever you go, there you are. Here I am, dealing with the same garbage, albeit less of it, in a different form. It's the same ignorance from living in a bubble though. He thinks nothing could ever go wrong in Hale Kapua. Except for an outbreak buoyed by genetic defects due to inbreeding. The island is small."

KC's therapist agreed.

"He would never choose me over his family," KC said. "Not that I would ask him to. Or want him to. I barely know him. I'm saying it out loud because logically, that makes sense. I met Lo five months ago. I spent over half that time dating Alvester. I've only been on three actual dates with Lo, plus a couple of days ago when I dumped him.

"It doesn't make sense to trust someone so quickly. Because I don't trust myself. That's why I've felt so confused."

KC sat up. "My instincts are drawing me to Lo, but the memory of my past failures won't let me take the risk. I want to believe. I can't.

"I guess I left him before he could leave me. I wanted the power. I'm in control. I decide."

KC frowned. "Now I'm unhappy for a different reason."

She spotted the clock: 1:50.

KC grabbed her bag. "See you next week!"

51. So this is Christmas... Eve.
Wed night, Dec 24, 2014.

"Is it time for gifts?"

KC watched a jittery Shira patrolling the blinking tree in Swan's living room.

"But it's not tomorrow yet," Shalom said, finishing her lime sorbet at the dining room table.

"Some families open one gift on Christmas Eve," KC offered, taking her plate to the sink. "One gift per person, not one total."

"I have one gift per person," Shira announced. "For all of you."

"I like gifts," Miguelito said, as he cleared the rest of the table. "I'll open mine."

Shira looked to the head of the table at Swan for approval.

"Huh?" Swan was distracted by the *Current Messenger* article that she was scrolling through on her phone. "Go ahead." She rolled toward the tree.

Shira entered the hall closet to retrieve five bulky boxes, each wrapped in different metallic paper and a matching bow. She hefted each box to its respective recipient, until she reached Swan.

"Why did they waste all this time?" Swan asked.

"It's a blanket?" Sitting on the bamboo floor, Miguelito held up a copious swath of fabric, half of which was still pooled in the box.

"They're quilts." KC examined her gift, constructed of ballet pink-flowered patches.

"I made them in your favorite colors," Shira said with hopeful pride, still holding Swan's present. "Or, I had them made, traditionally crafted in the local style," she clarified, peering at Swan, who remained glued to the article.

In an overstuffed club chair, Poobah ensconced his body in his green-patterned quilt. "Aren't you going to open yours?" he asked his daughter.

Swan kept reading.

KC spied the headline over her friend's shoulder. "The capital is moving to Lake Elmo."

"As originally planned," Swan confirmed.

Shira gently removed the phone from Swan's hand, exchanged it for her gift, and read the news herself. "Whaaat?"

Swan untied her bow before peeling off the wrapping paper. "It does say 'Ohana Circle will expand as planned. So there's that. And there is more room in the Northern Territory, and newer infrastructure to build upon."

"And a more competent mayor," Miguelito said, scrutinizing his sky-blue patchwork. "This is big. Now I won't have to pack it."

"We're saved," Shalom muttered from behind her book. She was lounging face up on the area rug in the center of the room, covering herself with her yellow quilt. "Hooray. Thank you, Shira."

Placated by her recipients' responses, Shira sat next to KC on the couch. "What does that mean for you and Lo? It would be nice to keep both of you on the committee in a functioning manner."

Swan said nothing and looked away, but waited for an answer.

KC covered her lap with her pink flowers. "I don't know."

52. Boxes, not boxers.
Fri morning, Dec 26, 2014.

"That's one mix plate, a manapua, a kimchi, and macaroni and cheese pancakes, for KC, to go?"

"That's correct."

"It'll be right out."

"Thanks, Kaina."

KC found an empty stool at a tall table near the counter at Kau Kau. With her cheek resting on her fist, KC noted that the restaurant was busier than she'd expected.

The back screen door opened and shut with a bang. A murmuration of guests entered the room. Some of the new diners looked vaguely familiar to KC, so she greeted her acquaintances with a "Good Morning."

But when the crowd formed an organized queue to place their orders, KC saw two people she hadn't recognized before sitting at a booth in the back.

Lo and Snow Belle.

Before anyone else could see her, KC slinked her way to the Wahine's room. Inside, she saw that one of the two wooden stalls was occupied by two small brown feet wearing ballet pink sandals.

KC crossed her arms. She made sure that she would be able to hear her name through the door.

As she began to occupy herself by washing her hands, KC heard sad sniffles coming from the occupied stall.

KC tiptoed over. "Hello?"

The sniffles stopped.

"Is something wrong in there?"

KC waited a moment. She didn't hear anything. So she stepped away slowly.

"Yes," a small voice said.

KC stepped forward. "What happened?"

Another sniffle, followed by sobs. "I had my period, and I didn't know, and I didn't bring a pad, because I forgot, because I had my first period last month, and I didn't know when it would come again because no one told me." More sniffles.

"Should I go get someone? Are your parents here?"

"No! My dad doesn't know what do."

"It's okay." KC set her purse on the sink counter to paw through it. "I have a pad. It might be a little big, but would you like me to hand it to you?"

Sniffle. "Okay."

KC stooped down and held out the pad, which was retrieved by a small, brown hand with chipped glitter polished fingernails.

"Thank you."

"You're welcome." KC kept listening for her name outside. Nothing yet.

The stall swung open.

Nala walked out.

Both she and KC gawked at each other, stupefied.

Nala, still regarding KC, washed her hands. "Don't tell my dad."

KC stepped aside to let Nala dry her hands with the paper towels. "I won't."

"Okay." She walked out of the bathroom.

KC, still in shock from her encounter with a pubescent tween, waited a moment, then exited the bathroom, and hid in the hallway, until her name was called.

"KC?"

She saw Lo look up from his tray, but KC grabbed her greasy bag from the cashier and scurried out of the restaurant before Lo could lock eyes with her.

Safely outside on the sidewalk in the bright sunshine, KC enjoyed a moment of pride about her escape.

Then, grudgingly, she sent an obligatory text before the next bus arrived.

"Yep."

53. Take a cup.
Wed night, Dec 31, 2014.

"Everything is so good."

"We needed more of these on the road."

At the New Year's Eve luau at Big Beach, KC stood with Vin at the outdoor buffet table under the stars, grazing from the fruit and vegetable arrangements.

"I thought on the tour it would be all produce, all the time," KC mused, before devouring a cup of mango chunks.

"It would be if I left the meals and snacks up to my business partner," Vin said, after swallowing a slice of kiwi. "But papayas, pineapples, and avocadoes aren't as easy to find in other Homestead communities as they are here on the island."

"We are truly blessed."

"So we compromise for time and eat what's available and circle the Southern hemisphere to hit all our stops in less than a month. Ooh, that's my song!"

Vin joined a group of partygoers on the dancefloor in the Electric Slide, leaving KC at the table.

After drifting through the buffet, surveying the tropical offerings, and landing on a shrimp ceviche, KC looked up to see a crew of well-dressed male friends enter the function a few yards away from her. In the center of the bromantic bunch was Lo.

KC let go of the fish dish and locked eyes with him.

Neither one of them moved.

Neither one stopped staring at the other.

Vin returned to the table to see KC and Lo standing on opposite sides of the party, arms crossed, frowning at each other, refusing to budge.

Vin plucked a champagne flute from a passing tray. "Why don't you go over there?"

KC kept glaring at Lo. "Why doesn't he come over here?"

Vin sipped her beverage. "Didn't you tell him you wanted space?"

KC unfolded her arms. She rolled her eyes and walked toward the other side of the event.

Lo's face relaxed into satisfaction, smug from winning the battle.

"Happy belated birthday," KC choked out.

"One year older, one year wiser," Lo said. "Thanks for the text, by the way."

"It was the right thing to do."

"I didn't tell Nala, but she told me, unprovoked, that KC is 'not so bad.' That's high praise from Nala."

"How was the tour? Vin said she had a nice time."

"I missed you."

KC had to look away as Lo's gaze bore into her soul. "I missed you too."

"Then why'd you break up with me?!" Lo whined louder than he expected.

"It's hard to explain."

Lo groaned. "I have an idea of what's going on, especially after I ran into Shira a couple days ago."

"What did she say?"

"She mumbled something about a red door, and then she mentioned that you seemed more relaxed now that the capital's moving to Lake Elmo."

"Yeah..."

"Were you mad about what I wrote?"

"Yes."

"Why didn't you tell me?"

"We were dancing," KC demonstrated one of the eight counts, "and I forgot, and then I remembered, and I got confused."

"About what?"

"I felt so happy with you and your family and your friends. And your food. But none of you knows what it's like... You all feel so secure here, like Hale Kupua is untouchable. You don't know."

Lo reached out his arms, then put them down, then lifted one arm tentatively in KC's direction.

"You can hug me."

Lo did. "It won't happen here. At least not today. I made sure of that. I hope I did."

KC pulled back "What?"

"On the Australian leg of our tour, I met with Mia to discuss our mutual interests."

"What?"

"We only talked. Upright. In a conference room. Vin was there, and some other witnesses. We're franchising The Movement Center in Lake Elmo to train the TV and movie talent."

"Congratulations."

"And... to make a long story of extended negotiations short, we pulled strings to get Kapualani Ranch and 'Ohana Circle all the funding requested without being the capital, under Mia's purview. She doesn't care about the money; she wants the prestige, the consolidation of power."

"Somebody else's problem. Why'd you do it?"

"I want you to feel safe. Also, you made valid, passive aggressive points for me to mindread. And I want to end this curse."

They both looked happier.

"I'm not leaving." KC looked at the throng of partygoers doing the Cupid Shuffle. "Would you like to dance?"

"I've danced nonstop for four weeks straight. I'd rather sit with you somewhere quiet and hold your hand."

KC sent a text and waved bye to Vin, who replied with a thumbs-up from the dancefloor.

"Let's go."

"Where?" Lo asked.

"I thought you knew."

"The twins are at a sleepover until noon tomorrow."

"Do you have any food I will eat?"

"Kau Kau delivers."

KC took Lo's hand. *"Allons-y!"*

54. Now and then.
Sat afternoon, July 04, 2015

"And we lived happily ever after with no problems at all!"

Outside, the sky was pouring rain on the pavement, but the sun kept on shining through the office windows.

KC smiled at her therapist. "Not really. Though I do feel so much better than I have in a long time. It's amazing how the past six months has evolved. The whole year, even.

"I have a team. Well, I'm on a team. Two other people. An office manager. And a Director of Infrastructure for 'Ohana Circle, who is dealing with all of the crusty boxes on our floor that aren't labeled 'Business Development.' Work has become so much easier and productive and less overwhelming and confusing. I love working together to make our town better. Teamwork!"

KC shook her head as she recalled the past. "I was so bummed out a year ago. Justifiably. I'm still angry about what happened to all of us. But that wound is healing. I found peace. Which was the mission of the Associates in the first place.

"And Red Spore won't be harming us again anytime soon. At least in their previous iteration. Mayor Berger let me know that the two leaders of the troops who terrorized us were convinced to flip, and now they're both working in Counterprogramming in Naboombu. The rest of the organization disintegrated.

"Finally, I can enjoy the charmed lifestyle we were trying to spread to others. I feel connected to my 'Ohana Circle community. I do miss my old family. I wish they could meet my new family.

"In 12 months, I haven't let anyone except Swan inside my apartment. But that changes today. I'm hosting an early family dinner."

KC nodded at her therapist's astonishment. "Yes, right after our session. Lo is coming over early to help set up. It will be his first time walking through my door.

"Which sounds suspicious, because I've been at his apartment or his parents' house or some other of his family members' houses every week this year. But I wanted to take my time. We have been open and honest with our communication. We're growing together. We're on the same page. Very much thanks to you!"

The clock struck 1:50.

"Therapy is awesome. That's what I tell all my friends now." KC ambled toward the exit. "They already knew."

Before she left, KC spun around to ask one more question. "Can I keep coming, even though I'm fixed?"

55. Knock knock, ding-dong.
Sat afternoon, July 04, 2015

"It's open!"

"I can't enter unless you invite me in!"

KC, who was wearing a pink seahorse Aloha shirt and denim capris, hit the pause button on her laptop. She bounced off the couch to her front door, jostling a basket of craft supplies off a pillow.

"Come in, please," she told Lo, who was holding something behind his back.

"Are you sure?" he said, from the hallway.

"I am giving you enthusiastic consent."

Lo peeked his head in. His eyes scanned the visible areas of the apartment. "No crazy detected."

"It's well hidden." KC kissed his nose and closed the door behind him. "You're dry. Did it stop raining?"

"A while ago. But I still got wet."

"Me too."

"Am I the first to arrive?" Lo noticed the open computer on the coffee table. "What are you watching?"

KC flicked her curls off her face and pressed play. "I'm trying to honor the traditions of our Pacific Islander culture." On the screen, a woman sitting at a beachside picnic table demonstrated how to make your own lei.

"How's that going?"

KC delved through a nearby bin containing plumerias, tuberose, carnations, and orchids. She retrieved a long piece of fishing line strung through a handful of irregularly placed blossoms. "Here's my first one."

Lo set his package on the table so that he could place the scraggly lei around his neck. "Festive."

KC departed to her bedroom. She returned carrying a stack of white cardboard boxes piled higher than her forehead. "Take that off."

Lo watched KC dump the boxes on the couch.

She replaced her previous creation with a fluffy pikake and pakalana garland, full of expertly linked white and green flowers. "That's better. I should have just left it to the professionals. Is that for me?" KC reached for Lo's package.

Lo nodded as she peeled off the wrapping. "Happy housewarming."

Sitting among the stray flowers, KC radiated joy at his gift, a framed photo of KC with Lo, his daughters, and his parents at the farm.

Lo sat with KC. "Hey."

"Yeah?"

He held on to her free hand. "I love you, Kharisma Celeste."

"I know."

"How do you know?"

"You've been telling me every day since I said it to you first, on New Year's Eve."

"It's still true."

KC rested her head on his shoulder. "We should snog for a bit before the other guests arrive."

"Okay."

Before they could go too far, there was a knock at the door.

KC disengaged from their embrace.

Lo adjusted his lei. He headed for the kitchen and opened the refrigerator to take out the prepared vegetable dishes.

"Hey."

"Yeah?" Lo replied to KC.

KC closed the refrigerator door. She pulled Lo's body close to hers, pressed her cheek against his, and nibbled his ear. "I love you."

KC walked out of the kitchen, leaving Lo standing on the tile floor, dazed, but delighted.

"We're here!"

"Happy anniversary to us." Shalom gave KC a hug.

Shira arrived behind Shalom, carrying a jollof rice dish.

"We made this together," Shira told KC as she received her professional lei.

KC anointed Shalom with her flowers as well. "I look forward to eating it."

"We made it together," Shira repeated.

"You mentioned that," KC said.

Shalom gave Shira a friendly pat on the back and took the container to Lo.

KC closed the door. "Where's the rest of—"

There was another knock.

Swan, Poobah, Miguelito, Vin, Snow Belle, and Nala all arrived at the same time.

"We didn't plan this," Swan told KC, before she could ask.

Shalom helped distribute the rest of the leis.

"Where are Tutu and Tutu?" Lo asked his daughters about his parents.

"They told us to come upstairs to get you to help them," Snow Belle replied, waiting impatiently for her lei.

Ahead of Snow Belle, Nala was mesmerized by the teenager who was giving her flowers. She kept asking Shalom questions to remain in personal space.

Snow Belle eventually grabbed a spare lei, placed it over the ringlet fauxhawk on top of her head, and made her way to the hors d'oeuvres.

"I'll go down with you," KC told Lo.

As Lo and KC moved toward the door, Nala briefly tore her attention away from Shalom. "Nice place," she told KC.

Lo looked wary, but KC said, "I do try."

Downstairs, KC and Lo met Lo's parents outside as they

rolled food containers up the damp walkway.

"We're so happy to be here." Ms. Hobbs gave KC a kiss on each cheek.

"Carry this for your mother," Mr. Gambon told Lo, passing him a cart topped with a bowl of kalua pork. "And carry this for me."

"You didn't have to bring anything," KC told them, holding the double doors open for the three of them to enter. "But we will eat it."

As she guided them in, KC looked up toward the road and saw a jogger traveling up the sidewalk in yellow shorts and conspicuously expensive running shoes.

"Speak for yourself," Lo said, to the meat bowl.

The jogger slowed down at the end of the walkway to stretch his sculpted beige calves.

Mr. Gambon cleared his throat at his son's insolence.

KC stared at the jogger, until he saw her too. He stopped stretching.

"And speak for me too," Lo told KC, while looking at his father. "Yum yum, eat 'em up."

KC squinted to confirm she was seeing what she thought she was seeing.

"That's what I thought." Mr. Gambon followed his wife into the building.

The jogger hiked up the path toward the entrance.

Her anxiety rising, KC gripped the metal handle of the open door.

Finally noticing his girlfriend's discomfort, Lo put down

the food carriers and placed his hand on her shoulder. "What's wrong?" He spotted the strange man closing in on them. "Hello there?"

KC took a step backward.

The stranger's light blue-green eyes were fixed on his target. "KC?"

KC stood still. "Topher."

FIN

Other Books by Mahlena-Rae Johnson

Steve the Penguin
(https://www.amazon.com/Steve-Penguin-Mahlena-Rae-Johnson/dp/0979935709)

Bianca Reagan: Where the Action Is
(https://www.amazon.com/Bianca-Reagan-Action-Mahlena-Rae-Johnson/dp/0979935717)

LAST MINUTE GUIDE to APPLY TO COLLEGE
(https://www.amazon.com/LAST-MINUTE-GUIDE-APPLY-COLLEGE-ebook/dp/B01L2HJT9W)

About the Author

MAHLENA-RAE JOHNSON grew up on the mean beaches of St. Thomas, Virgin Islands. During her senior year of high school, she was named Most Likely to Kidnap a Backstreet Boy.

After graduating from the School of Film and Television at Loyola Marymount University, Mahlena decided to stay in Los Angeles to crawl up the ranks of the entertainment industry. In 2007, Mahlena founded Mr. J Media and published her first novel, *Steve the Penguin.* She later elected to continue her overeducation by going to business school and getting her MBA at the University of Southern California.

Mahlena published her second novel, *Bianca Reagan: Where the Action Is*, in 2013, and then published her third book, *LAST MINUTE GUIDE to APPLY TO COLLEGE* in 2016.

When she isn't gorging herself on reruns of *Murder, She Wrote* and *The New Adventures of Old Christine*, corralling her growing family, or wondering what she should do with her MBA, Mahlena is working on *The Best of Everything*, a YA series about child genius orphans at a tropical island boarding school. You can read more of Mahlena's deep musings and witty quips at **Mahlena.com** (http://www.mahlena.com/).

Acknowledgments

Thank you to my family—the Hufflepuffs, the Gryffindor, and the ones who have neither read nor viewed any Harry Potter properties—whose love and support fill my Ravenclaw life with joy.

CPSIA information can be obtained
at www.ICGtesting.com
Printed in the USA
LVHW08s2108280818
588394LV00011B/1212/P